THE CARPATHIAN SHADOWS

Volume One

Edited by Lea Schizas

Stories by: William Koonce, Eric Keith,
Marcia Berneger, and Charles Mossop

**Books
ForA
Buck.com**
ePublishing

THE CARPATHIAN SHADOWS:

VOLUME ONE

Edited by Lea Schizas
Stories by: William Koonce, Eric Keith, Marcia Berneger, and Charles Mossop

Published by **BooksForABuck.com**

ISBN: 978-1-60215-061-4

CONTENTS

Foreword

Vampires, werewolves, zombies... all legendary creatures hunting their preys, all containing their own personal tales and backgrounds.

But the most evasive story to be told is that of Lord John Erdely from the Carpathian Mountains in Romania, Transylvania.

Lord John Erdely lived in the 17th century and date of death cannot be confirmed since no body has ever been found. It is rumored, but no documents support this theory, that he dealt in black magic to suppress the ongoing collaboration of the churches to bring a unified religion to all people, a Greek Catholic practice.

It is also rumored he may have used black magic to contain his servants, to blind and deafen them from words spoken to them while on errands for the Lord within the village of Cornifu. Villagers became increasingly suspicious of Lord Erdely when family members went missing.

Enter the present time...

All visitors staying in Cornifu Hotel are surprised with a mystery invitation for a one-day excursion to Erdely Castle. Befuddled but amused at the same time, they accept, unaware of the events to follow.

Join our characters as each discovers secrets and mysteries that will change their lives forever.

Lea Schizas
William Koonce
Eric Keith
Marcia Berneger
Charles Mossop

Arminius
By
William Koonce

There is no ill omen the equal of an assassin's contract. Someone must die. If not the name on the contract, then the assassin's life will do. Perhaps that serves as motivation superior to bounty. The assassin must be devoted but not fanatical. The nuance is one of emotional degree—devotion can elude passion while being pragmatic. The profession of an assassin is anything but perverse—it is an honorable profession, where dedicated men and women hone their craft to the same high standard a manufacturer does when building surgical instruments that slice flesh from navel to sternum. There is no self-reproach in the assassin's mind—in the end, it is the coroner's knife that makes the final cut.

Shortly after the evening news ended, a man gave up the relative comfort of a hotel bed and walked to a 3-drawer table next to the room's window. He grappled with closing the curtains over the expansive window and then thought otherwise; the seventh floor offered all required anonymity. He opened the table's top drawer and pulled out a singular photo. Taken from a great distance, the image was sharp and crisp. A scribbled name ran along the thin, white border.

Dorothy McNally.

She is pretty, he noted. He found blonde women attractive. The photo showed her staring straight at him, as if she sensed his presence.

Dorothy McNally owned 126 acres of prime farming land in Iowa that buttoned up to a string of north sprouting gambling casinos. Her finger-shaped farm almost touched the Missouri river. Gambling interests had exhausted their northern flank and they badly needed Dorothy's land for expansion.

The casino had offered Dorothy money for her land, an inflated offer. No price tempted her. The assassin used the last offer to boost his own fee. In retrospect, he wished he had asked for more.

He placed her photo on the table and turned his attention to the outside world. The picturesque, nighttime Omaha, Nebraska skyline stood before him. The Missouri River was a few miles east, and then Dorothy's farm. A wave of opulent self-satisfaction washed across his face; it seemed appropriate to be so high above the city, staring down at its occupants. Empty lives, he told himself—strip away the counterfeit smiles, remove the stylistic metaphors and what's left were spiritual vagabonds, useless and fake lives; echoes of youth and perpetual regret. At times like these, he actually felt he was doing the most good—ridding the world of obstacles. His thoughts drifted to Dorothy. He wondered if she were gazing now, into the night, laughing at her own situation. Doubtful. Most likely, she was staring, like him, into the night sky, reaching up and touching the secrets of her own soul as if omniscient, for she seemed to know all that she wanted.

He turned away and picked up the American Paranormal Association of World Tours packet that lay next to the photo. Dorothy was a member. A ticket to Transylvania, Romania, via cruise ship, plane, and train, was in one pocket.

The trip was just a glitch in his budget. Actually, not even that. The cruise wasn't necessary for those in the Paranormal Association, rather an option. His research of Dorothy's past exposed habits: each year she took the same cruise out of Boston on her way to Romania. Thus far, his research had been unable to identify her Boston hotel. No need to panic, he assured himself. There were other ways to track his prey. His instructions were to kill her in Romania. His faceless employer felt the local authorities would more easily identify a death as an accident. Too many cruise ship deaths generated questions best left unanswered. Accidents in his profession were contracts well fulfilled. His instructions neatly matched his own inclination.

The next day he left Omaha for Cruiseport, Boston and camped everyday in Black Falcon Cruise Terminal, located in the Boston Marine Industrial Park. He waited until Dorothy arrived to pick up her paperwork, recognizing her instantly from the photo.

When she left the terminal, he followed her on foot until the congestion seemed to thin near Seaport Boulevard. *Why so far away from the port*, he wondered. She certainly didn't seem to mind the seven-mile walk to reach her hostel.

Her bungalow was part of the Banana Bungalow chain. The rooms were clean and tightly decorated. The hostel was strictly no frills and catered to the young social crowd, with a host of activities centered on the beach.

He left his luggage in a dorm-like room and walked to a common area to observe. When he spotted Dorothy, he would wait a few minutes and follow. He did this for several days.

He became piqued when she brought a young man with a surfer tan to her room the night before the cruise. In the universe, nothing bothered him more than variables that spawned entropy. The tan man was an unknown quantity that might lead to chaos. Moreover, if for some last minute decision this man was to accompany Dorothy on the cruise...well, the assassin couldn't let that happen.

Later that night, he returned to the lobby of the hostel and using one of the open-booth phones, called her room.

"Ms. McNally."

"Yes."

"You have a package at the desk."

"A package? What is it? Who is it from?"

"Ma'am, I don't know...possibly a cake. Anyway, it needs to be signed for."

The line went silent for a moment as muffled conversation followed on her end. Then, "I'll come over and get it."

That's what the assassin wanted. *Come and get it, Dorothy.*

He made his way to her room and knocked.

"Who is it?" The tan man had his mouth close to the door.

"I have a package for Ms. McNally."

The voice on the other end sounded agitated. "She just left to pick it up, Slick."

"Will you sign for this, sir?"

"Slick...didn't you hear me...?"

"The box is cold, sir. It might be a cake."

After a moment's pause: "Okay...yeah...I guess so." The door's lock clicked and the assassin kicked it in.

Years earlier, the assassin had used a stun weapon on a target with a high tolerance for electrical stimulation. The target refused to go down and offered more fight than wanted. The assassin replaced *that* stun gun with one almost twice as powerful. The new weapon not only disrupted the signals within the nervous system, it forced the muscles to contract until the target was in the fetal position.

The tan, young man coiled and contracted to the floor like a spring tightening. Fortunately, hostel's—especially those catering to the youthful—tended to be clamorous with laughter and shouting. No one noticed the short cry of shock. The assassin quickly choked his victim into unconsciousness. The evening dusk provided cover as the assassin hoisted the man onto his shoulders.

Back in his room, the assassin opened a small, dark bag and withdrew a syringe. With practiced efficiency, he medicated the unconscious man, and after covering the pierced skin, stood, satisfied. *This will keep you out of my way.* He relaxed with drink and cigarette in hand, looking forward to the cruise; it was time someone waited on him; still, it would be a working vacation. He thought of Dorothy and the ship: a slip, a fall, a splash; however, that type of happenstance wasn't in his plans. She would die in Romania.

He figured she was back in her room now, perplexed about the young man's disappearance. She would spend most of the evening looking for him if only to return his clothes. Since the cruise was tomorrow, it was highly unlikely she would pick up another companion.

Relieved, he decided it was safe to stop for the day. Tomorrow, he and Dorothy would board the cruise ship. Pricks of excitement flooded over him like a hot bath as he contemplated getting closer to her. He finished off a glass of vodka, but didn't refill it. Alcohol made amateurs of assassins.

* * * *

A few extra bills above the normal rate got him a room next to hers on the cruise ship. The shared verandah made it easy to time his exit from his room with hers and strike up a conversation. Both gazed over the ship's rail, as if neither noticed the other.

"You can never get tired of a cruise," he said aloud and immediately regretted the remark, remembering that his last cruise resulted in a sunken ship and thousands of lives lost.

Dorothy only briefly acknowledged his presence, and then turned her attention back to the approaching sea. "Really," she said, picking up the conversation. "Which cruise line is your favorite?"

He was stuck, caught by his own stupidity. A sip from his afternoon tea gave him time to think.

"I have to admit," his stare bore into her, his remark timed so perfectly that perhaps serendipity lived after all, "with the view I see now, this one will end up being my favorite." He smiled, showing off his perfectly capped teeth.

She blushed, apparently forgetting her question, and pointed out, to small ocean swells that floated on forever, disappearing over the horizon. "It's like looking at eternity." Bashfully, her small mouth twitched when she realized he still stared at her.

He liked what he saw. He hadn't noticed her dark blue eyes until now. Framed by blonde hair, they floated on a light complexion. Her delicate features only made her appear more vulnerable.

She seemed uncomfortable. "Maybe...I should...return to my room and see what's on today's itinerary."

He thought of the tan man back at the hostel and found her feigned innocence almost entertaining.

"May I join you?" Why not be abrupt, he thought, if she was willing

8

to hop in bed with a beach bum, why not a stranger on a ship?

"Join me?"

"Share some of the ship's festivities with you."

"I...I don't know you," she said, shrinking away. "We may not like the same things."

He laughed inside. She was good.

"Would life be exciting if we did?" He could tell by her reaction that his question had become a bridge. She no longer had to be disingenuous, no longer demure. "Are you with someone?"

"No," she answered. She glanced up at his tall figure, enveloped in his shadow. She asked if he had come alone.

"I had plans to be with someone." Not entirely a lie. "It just didn't work out. I had already booked, so I decided I would go by myself. Actually, I hoped I would get fortunate and meet a lovely lady."

She smiled, apparently wanting him to continue.

"My name is Luther Hudson."

She held her long-nailed fingers up and shook his hand. "Dorothy McNally."

After several minutes of removing precautionary barriers, they both agreed to meet for dinner with the others from the paranormal group who had taken the same cruise.

Before dinner, Luther went to the one of the many shops on the ship and bought some cologne. He paid in cash, leaving the cashier a tip for also recommending a Zino Davidoff cigar. He appreciated a good smoke and the accompanied relaxation fine tobacco offered. The attendant gushed over the large tip and began chatting about nothing of any importance.

His field of expertise had taught him many things about people, especially women. He could have used his charms—he knew he was handsome—to perk her interest even more, but his interests rested solely on Dorothy. Still, he decided to spend some time talking.

"Thank you,"—her shiny gold nametag read Brandy—"you've made this an enjoyable purchase. "You're a lovely lady," though she was hardly much more than normal. "I noticed that as soon as I walked in—"

She blushed. Apparently, compliments about her looks weren't common. Truth be said, she could stand to lose some weight; still, she was good on the eyes.

"—and couldn't resist letting you know." Presently, he was the only patron in the store, so he relaxed and spoke with her at length. Did she enjoy her job, what were her goals?

In his line of work, he relished the opportunity to forget what he did for a living: kill people. Letting others talk about their selves helped him pretend he was like them. After several minutes of back and forth idle chitchat, he realized Brandy had become overly enamored with him. *Perhaps another day* he told himself. This cruise was business. He terminated the conversation.

That evening, dinner with Dorothy and her paranormal friends was excruciatingly dull. A few of her acquaintances were particularly annoying.

"Ghosts and goblins are the genesis of man's need to hope that more awaits beyond a life that meant so little. Genius really," a fat British man said, a smug arrogance surrounding him like the fat that covered his sinking jowls. Luther wondered if the old boy strained to sound overly British. "Invent what can't be proved so you can go about proving what you invented—simple and typical lives trying to be mysterious and atypical."

Dorothy smirked before replying. "Oh yes. See 'em prattle over nothing. Watch 'em see ghosts where none exists. Just dumb 'ole folk, uneducated and hope'n for some revelation." She looked hard at the now indignant man. "Is that all we are, just ole' dumb folk who are lucky to have you to enlighten us."

"Now see here, young lady—"

Luther sat up. Perhaps "the Brit" and Dorothy would make things interesting.

"Do you think everything can be explained away?" she interrupted.

"Why…yes. I do…from Christianity to Krishna, just man's imagination going amuck because of fear. *This* is all there is— he opened his arms wide "—and anything and everything can be explained."

"Then why are you here…on this cruise?" Dorothy asked.

"Isn't that obvious, my dear?" He smiled in triumph. "And that's your mistake…" He turned his attention to the entire table. "…everyone's mistake. I'm here because I wish to be--yet, you seem dumbfounded at the supposed incongruity of a man with my stance joining a paranormal group. You miss the obvious: I enjoy the entertainment." He laughed. "And that failing on your part is why you fall short when trying to explain the obvious, choosing instead to give the cause of your consternation a mystifying and supernatural quality. As I said, anything observed can be explained."

For the next several minutes, others at the table watched as the Brit and Dorothy took turns establishing their position, neither willing to budge. Luther sat motionless and said little. Still, he played the part as best he could and sometimes felt naked without something to describe as to why he had taken the voyage in the first place, but what could he say?

I'm here to kill Dorothy?

That thought made him laugh at just the wrong time.

"You find that funny?" The portly British man had the fork halfway to his mouth, the motion frozen as he waited for Luther's response.

Luther did a fast rewind. *There is so much evidence pointing to life after death.* That was about it...he hoped. He maneuvered his train of thought and responded.

"I don't find the idea of life after death funny. I just find it funny that the dead so often have no life while alive." His quip brought a roar of laughter from all and got him off the hook for the moment.

"That's so clever," Dorothy said, "and so true: so many live their lives in a state of safety that borders on—"

"—a living hell," Luther finished.

"Then you believe in a hell, Mr. Hudson?" An older, and thoroughly silicone and collagen pumped woman addressed him. It was obvious she had plenty of money to keep herself pretty and fit. He wondered if her husband had any idea that she was brushing her heels against a stranger's legs.

"No less than heaven, Mrs. Bradshaw." Luther tried to maneuver his leg out of the way.

"And do you," Dorothy asked Luther, "believe that there is a heaven?"

Luther didn't immediately answer.

"Come now, Mr. Hudson," the Brit interjected, "it seems everyone here but me believes in life after death. Surely, you—"

Luther had heard this before. The Brit droned on.

"—don't deny the existence of another dimension. Why, isn't that why everyone but me is here?" It was obvious the Brit was enjoying himself, possibly supposing he had a convert. "Aren't you here because you believe there is something more to death than the closing of a door, the last note in a song? There has to be something waiting for all of us beyond the veil."

Mrs. Bradshaw smiled. Her lips barely cracked as she spoke. "I don't think Mr. Hudson knows what he believes. He needs someone to show him." The tip of her shoe found the cuff of his paint leg.

What a bunch of idiots, Luther thought, each a victim of one thing or another, but most of all, victimized by their own lack of purpose. Perhaps he should kill them and let Dorothy live. *If only*, he wished.

"Let me ask each of you the same question," Dorothy said. "Is there a loving God who accepts us for who we are?" She waited a second and then, "Look at what most of the world has become: alone, tired, scared. Would any true God wish those attributes on anyone? I say no. So, let's continue to look for the dead and let them give us the answers."

The British man raised his glass, smiled as if offering a peace pipe, "Hear, hear. Well said." As Luther downed his European Cuvee Red, his thoughts drifted to the task at hand: do some killing. He and Dorothy shared mutual smiles as both laid their glasses down.

* * * *

The next evening, Luther was nursing a White Russian, determined to make it last until Dorothy arrived.

"Have you been waiting?"

He startled. It was unusual for anyone to sneak up on him.

"How did you sleep?" She asked.

"Like the dead."

He offered her a chair at the bar and, and after asking what she liked, ordered a Black Russian.

"Double," she said to the bartender.

Luther didn't resist his open approval but was opposed to having another one himself. Two White Russians in his unfed system would certainly dull his edge.

"Come now, Luther. Must I drink alone?"

He studied her expression and wondered just how far she would go tonight. Her short skirt suggested she didn't mind showing off lean, muscular legs. On the other hand, her buttoned blouse indicated she held modesty in reserve.

"Maybe during dinner," he replied.

* * * *

Later that night there was more discussion on the paranormal. Luther did his best to sound interested. Uncharacteristically, he ordered a third White Russian.

"Once we arrive in Romania," said Dorothy, "you will find Hotel Cornifu fascinating. It was renovated in the 1800's. Originally, it was a stagecoach-station. And guess what—"

Luther's face lit up, as if he were actually intrigued.

"—one of the things I would like to do—I hope you too—is head for the Meridionali Carpathian Mountains. Their local name is Transylvanian Alps."

He almost choked on his food. "As in Count Dracula?"

She smiled, amused at his reaction.

He swallowed the last of his dinner. If anything, the meal had made the evening bearable, but he couldn't count on the next meal doing the same thing. He became contemplative. For the next several days, he would need to stay close to Dorothy. Would he have sex with her? Should he? Would he regret it latter? Sure as hell, he would. As dangerous as it was, sex was necessary in his line of work. He couldn't allow someone else to hop into her bed, so to speak.

"So, should I bring along some garlic?" He asked.

She laughed. "Don't get caught up in myths and fables that have nothing to do with vampires."

"Good, I didn't bring my silver cross with me either."

"I was talking about garlic being the myth, Luther."

He stared at her.

She finally grinned and terminated the pregnant pause: "Everyone knows vampires don't exist, right Luther? Still, I find the subject fascinating."

He poured her another glass of wine from a carafe.

"Transylvania is the subject of my life, Luther. I've traveled to Romania countless times and each time I walk away different."

"How?"

"Revitalized…Romania is the most beautiful country in Eastern Europe. It's a place where medieval past exists in the present; a country imbued with life. It gives me meaning. Isn't that what you spoke of last night, at dinner? 'I just find it funny that the dead so often have no life while alive.' Well, I have a life, and Transylvania is part of that living—"

He could see the assertion coming.

"—and you'll feel it too."

She was right. Only he felt it now. He regretted the extra drinks. They clouded his mind and speech. They also sharpened his eyesight. She was more beautiful than he had noticed. He wondered about the short skirt and felt emboldened. Was it his imagination, or had she unbuttoned the top of her blouse.

"Time to dance," she said.

* * * *

The next morning, he woke with a slight hangover. After a shower and shave, he left his room only to find a note taped to the door. It was from Brandy.

That's all I need.

He read the scribbled lines and then put the note in his pant pocket. Things were getting out of hand. Complications.

A big breakfast helped him forget the hangover. He chastised himself for drinking and after some effort of memory, determined he had revealed nothing the previous night to compromise his position. As he pushed his plate away, he saw Brandy approaching. The good taste of eggs and sausage left immediately.

In Luther's line of work, uncertainties had to be limited. He had made a mistake flirting with her. Where could he run? A wall of ocean wreathed escape and the tide of uncertainty she offered demanded a swift termination. At the thought of looking like a cad, he smiled broadly upon her approach. No brush off this: he was a gentleman or nothing else. Remarkably, he did have a conscience. He would let her know he was with another woman.

"Good morning, Brandy."

"Mr. Hudson. I saw you eating alone and wondered if you wanted company."

He stood to pull out a chair. "Please." He waited for her to relax and then said, "Brandy, please accept my apology for leading you on. I should have told you that I'm with someone." He watched her pale blue eyes. They reflected little emotion, certainly no surprise. Her voice was as smooth as warm butter, showing no embarrassment as she spoke.

"Luther...a man like you always has women. I'm not that naive." She reached over and plucked the remaining sausage from his plate. After a few moments of silence, she continued. "The way I figure it is this: I've never gone for anything in my life, never wanted the brass ring. You made me want to take a chance." Her hand covered his. "Don't worry; I'm not going to stalk—"

"Am I disturbing something?"

Luther withdrew his hand.

Brandy barely acknowledged Dorothy as she spoke. "Yes, you are disturbing."

Dorothy seated herself across the table.

Luther's natural arrogance only heightened his intuition. There was going to be catfight over him and he would be much more comfortable sitting on a fence far away. The ease with which he had used both women came back to haunt him. Justice. His safest choice was to sit back and watch while they extended their nails and began scratching.

"Don't you think she's a bit young for you, Luther?" Dorothy asked, all the while smiling at Brandy.

"That's funny," Brandy replied. "I was about to remark about your...advanced age."

"He's out of your league, little girl," Dorothy snapped, elevating the confrontation to the next level.

Somehow, it seemed unrefined for Dorothy to speak that way, but Luther tried not to smile. When Brandy didn't follow suit, he formed a modicum of respect for her.

Brandy stood and turned her attention on Luther. "I'm not going away, Luther. You can do a lot better than...than this." She pointed at Dorothy. "Don't let her clever makeup fool you. She's a lot older than you think."

Dorothy stiffened. "I'll have you fired!" She spoke loud enough for others in the dining facility to take notice.

Luther didn't hesitate. "I'm out of here, ladies."

"Stay, Luther," said Brandy. "If she is what you want, I'll leave, but if you change your mind, you know where to find me. The ship isn't that big."

Luther breathed out slowly and deep as Brandy walked away. He had become extremely nervous, though he wouldn't admit it to himself. A man in his profession had to have cauterized nerves. He did admit that he resented Dorothy intruding like she did. In addition, was it just Brandy's power of suggestion or did Dorothy actually look a bit older this morning?

He tried not to tune Dorothy out as she mapped out the remainder of their time on the ship. He calculated the number of days until they reached port. It couldn't come soon enough. After that, he and Dorothy would fly to Bucharest, Romania, and then take a train to their final destination.

* * * *

The cruise ship arrived in Portugal early morning. After disembarking, Dorothy and Luther caught a flight to Bucharest. From there they traveled by train to a station three miles from Hotel Cornifu. A full top burgundy Barouche carriage waited when they stepped off the train. A blonde Belgium horse pulled the carriage. The coachman was a big man with black hair stuck to his forehead like a dark tattoo.

After accepting Luther's hand, Dorothy entered the carriage. Early morning rain was just beginning to fall, so both positioned themselves toward the middle of the plush, red seats. Cold seemed to mate with each drop.

Luther couldn't understand why she had insisted on taking the carriage to the hotel instead of accepting the transportation supplied by the Paranormal Association. When he realized he couldn't convince her otherwise, he had no choice but acquiesce.

Except for the hypnotic cadence of the horse's hooves on the cobblestone street, the ride was uneventful. Luther watched shingled, tiny homes pass by and marveled at the beauty of the hilly countryside with its numerous vineyards. Neither he nor Dorothy spoke much during the ride. Twenty minutes later, they arrived at their hotel.

The hotel clerk handed both he and Dorothy sealed envelopes upon checking in. Impatient, Luther put down his luggage and opened his envelope. Dorothy didn't seem to care, as if she already knew what the letter said. He read the letter aloud.

"Dear Mr. Luther Hudson:

We cordially invite you for a free tour within the famous castle of Lord Erdely.

Our guide, Jennifer Brooks, will be departing tomorrow at 8am sharp from Hotel Cornifu for this one-day excursion we have planned.

Visit the mysterious surroundings of the Erdely Castle and see for yourself if it is indeed haunted.

Yours truly,

Bruce Campbell
President of The American Paranormal Association of World Tours."

"What a lovely idea," Dorothy said.

"Aren't you going to open yours?"

"No...maybe later. I'm sure it's the same thing."

"I suppose you know about this castle...Lord Erdely Castle."

"A little," she said. "The castle is located in the Carpathian Mountains. There are stories...rumors really, that the castle is haunted."

Luther grabbed his luggage, as well as Dorothy's, and both headed for the elevator. "And this Lord Erdely?"

She pushed the button for her floor. He noticed her fingernails had lost their luster and age spots were appearing on the back of her hands. As the door closed, she answered.

"He appeared around the 17th century, but he was a man for all ages. He would have loved the United States."

"Why is that?"

"He hated organized religion; hated worse the idea that God's people might someday win."

"Win...?"

"Some great battle in the future. Lord Erdely's vision of the future was drastically different from that written in the Christian Bible. His Armageddon didn't end in God's victory."

Luther followed her through the elevator as its doors opened to her floor.

"And if he's wrong?"

"Lord Erdely didn't care," she replied. "He hated God and anything to do with Him."

"You're right."

"What's that?"

"He would have loved the United States."

She continued with her story.

"Lord Erdely was an atheist. Perhaps more precisely, he didn't worship the God of the Bible."

Luther looked at the passing room numbers. "I think this is your room." He patiently waited as she opened the door. The luggage was getting heavy. Then he said, "So, he was a religious man, just not the right kind." He watched her pause at the door's threshold.

"It depends on your perspective, Luther—his and yours." She scrutinized him as if suspicious. "You don't strike me as a religious man."

"I'm not. Everyone has his or her own opinion about God. I choose to have none."

She stepped aside, holding the door open, and stared intently as Luther entered before speaking.

"Even now, locals speak of his name in hushed tones."

He sat on the bed and stretched his back. "You don't seem to have that problem."

She ignored his comment and continued. "You'll find local yore accusing Lord Erdely of dabbling in the art of black magic."

"Did he?"

"History is not too specific. They say he used his knowledge to control others. Many of those visiting his castle reappeared in the village somehow changed. As if..."

For several seconds Luther sensed Dorothy struggling against a code of silence, and then she smiled, reserved. She seemed to have latched on to an appropriate response.

"As if what?" he asked.

"History is not too specific," she repeated, apparently finished now. Luther didn't feel obliged to prompt her for more, and the carriage ride had left him cold. A hot shower was what he wanted. He stood to leave.

He asked, "You want to get a bite to eat tonight after freshening up?" He enjoyed this display of familiarity; it provided comfort that no one else would step in to take his place. He was close now to his ultimate goal. Soon, someone was going to die. He just wasn't sure whom.

"Not really. I'm terribly tired," she said in a throaty tone, as if she were catching a cold. "I'll be asleep soon. You want to go together...tomorrow...to the castle?"

She did look weary. Luther thought of Brandy, what she had said. Dorothy did look years older and her makeup couldn't conceal that fact.

"Wouldn't miss it. I'll see you in the morning."

* * * *

The driver's name was Vlad Mysecki. He provided transportation for all the invited guests to Erdely Castle. When Dorothy refused the limousine and demanded she and Luther ride the horse drawn carriage again, he almost balked. The tour guide, a pretty 30'ish brunette, reminded Dorothy the entire group must stay together. Dorothy responded by asking where the invitation said that. She and the guide argued, and in the end, Luther decided he could either ride with the rest of the group and lose sight of Dorothy, or get wet again, for the previous day's rain had not abated in the slightest. For him, there was little choice in the matter. The horse's neigh seemed to warn him to hurry before the rainfall turned into a torrent.

The carriage's metal and wood body creaked as Dorothy and Luther entered, as if it too, like Dorothy, were aging. This time Dorothy chose to sit on the opposite side, facing Luther. He winced as prickly rain struck his face. No doubt the ride would be uncomfortable. He looked at Dorothy. What was her problem? Why the carriage? He thought of the others in the paranormal group, warm and dry.

As the horse plodded toward Erdely Castle, he surveyed the area. The harsh rain made viewing difficult, and the dark, substantial clouds blocked out the early morning sun, making it difficult to see the small homes that crowded the street. These homes were different from those he'd seen yesterday, each one dirty looking, but neat; little villas that seemed to grow dark with shadows as the carriage passed. He made out what he thought were faces that stared from slits in drawn curtains that faced the street. He understood their fear, but now each face was an irritation, a distraction. He turned his attention back to Dorothy.

He took notice that Dorothy continued to age at an accelerated rate. He gave a sort of half-smile as she glanced his way. Her lips had hairline fractures that extended like thin fins on an oval. Long bangs tried to hide scarecrow feet that adorned each eye. The rain that dripped on her face followed deepening smile lines around her mouth.

She seemed to notice his scrutiny.

"I'm just thinking of Brandy," he said. And that was partially true. "She didn't seem like the type that would...take her own life."

"Luther," Dorothy said, "...the little twit was unbalanced. Her suicide note said it all. It wasn't your fault that you broke her heart."

He swallowed hard. Dorothy might have been less blunt. Still, he had serious doubts about the suicide. One moment Brandy was alive, perhaps a bit needy for affection; the next moment she slit her wrists. It wasn't her company he missed: he certainly didn't feel any guilt. It was simply that he didn't believe she killed herself.

The horse lumbered forward for what seemed several hours. Luther thought of the tour bus and its dry occupants. The bus must have taken a different route. *Probably one with a paved road,* he thought. His body jolted as one of the carriage wheels slammed into another muddy rut. He found the incessant rain increasingly uncomfortable and was about to say something when Dorothy nearly jumped from her seat

"Luther! Look!" Dorothy pointed through the rain, toward the lightening that hung over Erdely Castle like glittering tassels. "Isn't it beautiful? And to think we're going to be inside soon. I've missed it so much."

He didn't lose the implication.

She's been to the castle, perhaps many times.

No wonder she didn't open the invitation back at the hotel. That certainly explained why she was familiar with the castle...and its dark secrets.

The castle perched on the mountainside like a vulture in its nest. Its frontal, gray facing was painted in shadows that blended into its surroundings like grafted skin; its foundation resembling igneous rocks formed from cooling magma.

He listened as she rattled on.

"I can show you the secret places—places where we can be alone." He had no doubt she was a scant insane. "Did you know Lord Erdely is both feared and adored by his subjects?" She spoke with admiration, the rain spitting from her lips and dropping to the carriage floor. "He is a great lord—"

"You mean was a great lord," Luther corrected, wondering what her response would be.

Her burst of laughter was instantaneous. Even the driver snickered. She drew back. "Was? Of course, silly, what did I say? It's the rain. It's the castle...it's you. Don't pay attention to my prattling."

He wondered how she could be so loquacious when they both were getting drenched. Doesn't she realize the rain is turning her makeup into colored slicks, her hair into matted tendrils?

"Drive faster!" she barked to the coachman."

Thank the stars, thought Luther. *Yes. Drive like a bat out of hell.*

The growing storm above fissured the darkening sky like a jagged clever. The rain whipped across the carriage and covered Luther like cold sweat.

"The others will think we're nuts," he remarked, gesturing at their soaked state.

"The others will never see us; I've made sure of that. I want you all to myself, Luther."

He smiled and said to himself. *And I want what you are leading me too.*

"Our driver will take us through a mountain pass and then we will navigate a water canal whose tide will take us to a portcullis."

She held her hand out to cup the rain. "The storm is perfect; the upper Prut and Siretul will be engorged by the rivers that transverse the Carpathian mountain. The flood will take us directly to a secret passage that will gain us entrance into the castle. Normally, we would need to hike up a cliff to gain entrance. Lord Erdely had his favorite subjects use that entrance."

"How do you—"

"—know? I told you, I travel here each year. It's like coming home."

Lightning fractured the sky once again. The mountain about them crowded with shadows that resembled dark chasms, each an abyss to a secret place. Luther noticed Dorothy's lips moving silently, her attention riveted to the castle.

"What is that you're saying?" he asked.

She snapped to face him, her eyes ablaze, staring though him as if he weren't there. He repeated his question.

She blinked and came out of her trance. "I... I was just reciting an ode. I always repeat it when I come here. Would you like to hear it?"

He nodded, all the while feeling his heart race. The killing would start soon; he just hoped he wouldn't be the victim.

"Wit my Lord's intent, let it be known
It is the bane of the grave to hold mercy,
Let the earth hold those so ignorant."

"What does it mean?" He asked.

"No mercy and life eternal," she roared through the rain. "No mercy and life eternal!"

The carriage came to a choppy stop. The horse neighed and bucked. The coach jerked forward and backward until the coachman gained control.

"We're here!" She almost pushed Luther out.

With the dark shadows that the storm allowed, Luther realized he would never have found the entrance to the mountain pass on his own. The natural geography exploited the cliffs and hid the entrance. That realization soothed his sensibilities. The nightmarish ordeal with Dorothy had been necessary. He *had* needed her to show him the way. Soon, he would find what he really came to kill. She took his hand and they both followed the coachmen on foot.

"Why is *he* coming?" Luther asked.

"I need him." It was a simple statement and she offered no further explanation.

Someone else to kill.

Several minutes later, and true to her word, they came upon a small boat tethered to a group of stones stacked in such a way as to form a natural altar. Luther was taken aback when Dorothy bite into the cusp of her hand. She wiped the blood that trickled from the wound on the altar and then repeated her ode.

"Quickly...into the boat," she ordered, as the coachman steadied it.

Luther straightened. "To where?"

"I already told you. Hurry! The water is up. The river's current will take us directly to the portcullis."

22

Thunder reverberated in the narrow passage and lightening reflected off the mountainside like bursts of heat off wet skin.

Luther stepped into the boat as the coachman looped the rope off the rocks. The flow of the river snatched the tiny craft and carried them further into the flooded passage. Dorothy continually repeated:

> *"Wit my Lord's intent, let it be known*
> *It is the bane of the grave to hold mercy,*
> *Let the earth hold those so ignorant."*

Anxious, Luther failed to hide his impatience. "How far does this take us? Dorothy! How far?"

She turned toward him. He cared little about the pronounced aging, but now…her face; it had a rage and hunger that seemed to banish from her countenance the very rain that now drenched him.

"Not far," she said. "Soon I will show you the secrets of Erdely castle."

Luther nodded. *Soon I will kill you, your coachman, and your master.*

* * * *

Torches burned at the entrance like sentries. A fortified outpost—a barbican—was carved into the mountain as they approached the portcullis. The barbican was intimidating, and in the past most certainly served to ward off intruders. As they exited the boat and headed for the entrance, Luther noticed a stone-lined cistern fed by water running off the mountain. It overflowed now, fed back into the rising river that sliced through the mountain. There was a red stain in the cistern. It had once held more than water.

"Come," Dorothy beckoned, removing one of the torches from its hold.

Luther followed her through the entrance and into the mountain with the coachman close behind. Once inside, a steep set of steps led up a narrow passage and to a postern gate. Footing was unsure, as the bedrock beneath their feet was damp.

At the top of the stairs, Dorothy swung the creaking gate open and they stepped into what Luther assumed were the bowels of Erdely Castle.

"Careful," she warned. "We're almost there."

The gate opened to a portico. When Luther hesitated, letting his eyes become accustomed to the new surroundings, the coachman nudged him on.

"Get your hands off me!" Luther contemplated killing the coachman where he stood.

The coachman smiled and retreated.

"Hurry!" Dorothy's voice was changing—older, weaker.

The three crossed a foyer that, though short, exhibited a high ceiling that stretched thirty feet up and before him now was a set of cathedral doors that used every inch.

The doors were magnificent in design and Luther immediately surmised they were entering a church from long ago. Designs in the door showed Biblical scenes—scenes from the Old and New Testament. Embedded in the door panels at various degrees were figures of past prophets. One prophet, positioned at the top of each door, was broken at the neck. It didn't take a holy man to realize that prophet was the Christ.

The coachman pulled on the massive doors.

Intrigued now, Luther stepped forward without any prompting. He entered a vestibule with confessionals on each side—although from the dust they hadn't been used in a long time. Once past the vestibule he came upon a huge basilica shaped, cavernous tabernacle. Thirteen tall, cylindrical columns adorned each side of the basilica, each displaying a recessed altar display with torchlight above. Below each altar display, chained to the columns hung skeletons—each decomposed to varying degrees. Twenty-six skeletons chained to columns in an underground church meant Luther had arrived. His real reason for selecting Dorothy was at hand.

He followed her as they all headed for the other side of the structure. He knew the coachman was close behind because the big man's foul breath stuck to his neck. Luther controlled his breathing, calming himself. *I mustn't panic.* He was almost to his goal. He could feel it.

As they walked the length of the long Roman-like tabernacle, his mind had time to idle. His thoughts returned, like scratch to itch, like child to mother, to a life long ago—a time where he'd known nothing of the sacrifice of Christ.

And so to his damned soul.

Over two thousand years ago, he had sold his soul to the darkness. At that time, he chose not to deeply contemplate his decision. He'd been, after all, Arminius, a great Germanic tribe leader. Still, time changed his perspective; a world of hate, deceit, lust, and death trapped him. What had happened?

One moment, the contest of life made things worthwhile. The next moment those things most important were handed to him on a platter, without struggle or merit. He became empty.

24

Many years later, a priest had approached him and spoke to that emptiness. He spoke of the filling that Christ offered, but there was a catch: One can't simply sell a soul to the Prince of Darkness and return to a normal life. To crucify Christ again, a price must be paid. If Arminius accepted in faith the death and resurrection of Christ, he would himself have to die. Instead of welcoming his own death, Arminius had used his bargaining skills and garnered a new task. He would roam the earth, fight evil in all its forms, and do this until the return of Jesus. For the past two thousand years, that's exactly what he'd done: fight evil.

Dorothy was evil. Luther knew what kind of creature she was, and whom she was taking him to see. Any pretense on her part had evaporated. She'd led her cow to slaughter and no longer cloaked her urgent need for what Luther could provide.

My blood is her milk. He understood her hunger well.

He heard her crazy ode in his head.

The three came upon a set of doors much smaller and less adorned than the previous door. This time, Dorothy opened one of the two doors. As Arminius had anticipated, the coachman jumped him, slammed him against the other door, put him in a chokehold, and then swung him around to face Dorothy. She approached and spat in his face.

"You thought you would kill me?" she asked, pleased with the new arrangement. "Not likely, you pathetic example of an assassin. Oh, yes. I know who you are. You thought the casinos hired you? What a fool. *I* hired you. It was the only way to get your here of your own free will."

Arminius calmed himself, choosing to wait for his moment. Let her rage.

"An assassin lives in anonymity," she continued. "No one notices when they disappear. That's why I chose you, Mr. Luther Hudson, assassin extraordinaire. And now you will die with no one in the world to miss you."

"Why did you have to kill the girl?" Arminius asked between clinched teeth, merely confirming what he already suspected.

"You mean your little tart on the ship? Why? Because she insulted me...telling me I was old." Like an aging actor who ignores the truth, Dorothy portrayed herself as something different. "I will live forever...young and beautiful always."

Arminius tried to smile, but only grimaced instead. The coachman's forearm was like a tree trunk against his neck. "Have you...looked in a mirror? You are...getting a little long in the tooth."

She snapped her yellow-nailed fingers at the coachman. "Bring him inside!"

25

Pushed past the door and into another room, Arminius didn't struggle.

A fire burnt against the far wall and torches rimmed the room's perimeter. On one wall hung portraits of monarchs and warriors with one exception, the most prominent picture was of Castle Bran, which still stands in the Carpathian Mountains. Vlad the Impaler, King of Romania, used it in 1456 - 1462, as a temporary residence.

Another wall displayed a painting of the Getae thunder god named Zalmoxis. Under that painting and sitting on ornate, oak shelves held numerous urns, each delicately decorated in family clan colors. This room was not only ancient, but held a prominent place in the castle's history.

A desk stood at the far end in front of the fireplace. Next to the desk, a man bent at the waist, dressed in shades of blue from head to foot stood with his back to Arminius. On the desk, a woman, her exposed legs kicking in rhythmic spasms, lay helplessly as the well-dressed man sucked at her throat. Another woman, an old woman like Dorothy, stood to the side, her tongue twitching against cracked lips. She was waiting, anticipating, struggling not to move. After the well-dressed man straightened, he motioned for the old woman to approach. She jumped forward and feasted on the nearly dead woman, sucking so harshly on the woman's neck that she appeared as a lapping dog.

The well-dressed man backed away, lit a cigarette, and admired his work.

As the old woman drank, her aging began to reverse. Hair, once gray, turned to a deep brunette. Wrinkled hands, pumping on the soon-to-be-dead woman's chest as if trying to siphon blood toward the wound, grew young: age spots disappeared, and jagged veins sank away.

The well-dressed man spoke. "Drink my darling. Be young again." His cultured voice held an old-world accent. He watched the hungry woman slurp and lick around the wound. It was easy to surmise that Dorothy was awaiting her chance, and that Arminius was the meal.

Without turning, the well-dressed man spoke. "So, what have you brought me, Dorothy?"

"Master," Dorothy spoke respectfully, her voice weak and feeble, her spine so bent she used the door for support. "I have..." she needed a breath "...brought Luther Hudson. Please take him...mingle your blood with his...let me drink."

The well-dressed man turned with a smile. He wore a loose cravat that seemed to diminish his polished look. His smile faded fast and transformed to astonishment and then the smile returned, followed by a simple statement that shocked Dorothy.

"This man is not Luther Hudson." The cigarette in his mouth glowed deeply as he inhaled. "This is Arminius."

Arminius squeezed out the well-dressed man's name: "Count Belarus."

At that moment, Arminius angled his right forearm—the one the coachman had pinned behind his back—in practiced fashion. A nine-inch blade sprang forth, its end locking in place at Arminius' wrist. The coachman gasped, released his grip. Arminius pulled his arm forward, and in doing so, removed the extended blade from the coachman's heart. He stepped aside and the coachman fell forward, dead. Arminius pointed the bloody blade at Dorothy and asked her if she wanted a lick.

Dorothy's eyes were nestled in dark sockets now. Her leathery skin hung on an old face. She stared at her former coachman's body—or was it his pooling blood she locked onto.

Belarus shook his head, as if disappointed.

"Dorothy," he spoke like a schoolteacher admonishing a pupil, "you brought the wrong man."

Strands of Dorothy's hair began falling to the floor. Her crooked nails clawed at the cold stone, her breathing raspy. "Please...master..."

"Do you know who this man is, my darling?" This time Belarus spoke to the rejuvenated woman, who had apparently finished with her meal.

The young, vibrant woman wiped fresh blood from her lips and shook her head no.

"This man is Arminius, the former chieftain of the Germanic Cherusci famous for their defeat of a Roman legion in the battle of the Teutoburg Forest. Only the victory was a bit tainted, wasn't it, Arminius? You lied to your people. They had no idea what really bought victory...and ultimately, destruction."

Arminius hesitated for several moments before answering. His conscience had long been frayed because of guilt and regret. His tattered soul was held together now by the love of Christ. He needed nothing else.

"I sold my soul to the Prince of Darkness for my tribes," he finally said. "The Romans were a plague consuming the land. We had to drive them out."

"So noble a cause was it?" Enquired Belarus. "Then why betray me?"

"Christ's sacrifice had not been made." Arminius answered. "I knew nothing of God. I was wrong. History shows my action only sowed devastation for my people—"

Belarus slammed his fist down onto the desk, at the same time violently shoving the dead woman to the floor. "The Prince of Darkness *was* your god! Curse you and your soul to hell for accepting Jesus as your path." Black hatred glared from his eyes. "Curse you for turning on me." He spat. "And curse your Christian faith."

With the skill of a man comfortable with speaking to creatures of the night, Arminius deflected Belarus' anger. "My soul was damned, but now I am free. I will, one day, be with Christ."

Belarus gave him a tiny tilt of the head. "Let me help you get there today, old friend." He smiled crookedly. "You will not escape this time."

He motioned at the crumpled body on the floor. "Do you remember sharing that? Drinking my blood mingled with that of a mortal, drinking the blood of life. With me, you would have lived forever."

"Yes, I remember, Belarus. I see the faces of those who died with my mouth at their necks, feeding on their blood as it trickled from the wound you left." He smiled dryly, intent not to let Belarus garner any edge. He would not let the past anchor him into inaction. The only regret would be if he failed now. He knew, no matter the difficulty, he knew he would kill Belarus. "I see those faces in my dreams. Still, Christ's sacrifice has cleansed me—"

"Do not mention His name again." Belarus blew a long cloud of blue smoke that hung in the air like a brewing storm. His animal eyes seemed to be contemplating their next move. "Arminius, I am not ignorant of what you've accomplished for the past thousands of years. You have hunted down many of my kind, murdered them, but you will find me not so easily killed."

He hasn't attacked me yet, thought Arminius. Why? His delay, his attitude; they were hints of something more. But what?

"You were among the first of your kind, Belarus. You've lived a long time, and I've search for you for many years. Hiding here, in Erdely Castle was wise; its evil shields even you. Lord Erdely had powers I have not yet unlocked; the evil that emanates from this castle, the black magic that its master practiced still clouds the mind of all who enter. When I realized you were here, I had to find a way to get to you." He looked at Dorothy. "So easy."

She hissed.

"Actually," Belarus said, "I've been expecting you for some time."

He inhaled deeply from his cigarette and then snubbed it in the palm of his hand. "Yes, it appears our Dorothy was quite the fool."

He dropped the cigarette to the stone floor and used a handkerchief to wipe clean his hand while smoke gushed from his nostrils like an enraged bull. "You turned your back on the cold and dark inner sanctum of the dead for an outside world that never appreciated you, and now you come here, back to my temple and threaten me."

His voice grew more menacing. "When I am through with you, Arminius, I intend to add to my stock from the paranormal group touring Erdely Castle. I am sure one or two will find the idea of immortality alluring."

"I will not let that happen," said Arminius, calm and serious. "Your abject life ends tonight."

"Does it? Will you and your God stop me? Will you save the others from immortality? Or will they live forever off my blood, bringing me victims so I may feed at my leisure? I will be their god, as I once was yours."

That arrogance and inactivity would give Arminius the advantage. Belarus had become lazy staying in his nest, waiting effortlessly to feed. His setup was perfect except for one thing: he had lost his edge.

Arminius waited.

"Tell me, Arminius, did you ever find your wife or child after your traitorous act of accepting God's love? Do you want to know what happened to them?" He didn't wait for a reply. "I do."

"Meaning?"

"Your son. Your wife. You deserted them."

"I did what was necessary."

"I'm sure they understood."

Arminius dropped a smile. "That was a long time ago, and if you think you can use them to—"

"Your worship at the Son of God's feet was a knife in their back...in my back. I recruited you for evil's sake. I even vouched for you in my master's presence."

"That's your problem."

"Is it? Let me explain something. You didn't find your wife, Thusnelda, or your son because I got to them first. You not only failed as a servant of darkness, but also as a husband and a father. Look at you—hunting those you once referred to as family. And you found me. And you intend to kill me." His fingers touched the chin of the rejuvenated woman. "And you too, my darling. All of us. Though it appears our poor Dorothy won't need Arminius' attention."

Dorothy continued to atrophy, her ineffectual pleas, only moans now.

"Tell me, Arminius, how did you find me? Did you take the place of Luther Hudson, or did the man never exist?" He laughed. "For years,

Dorothy has been bringing assassins to me. I mingle my blood with theirs and then she feasts, regains her youth. Now look at what you've done to poor Dorothy. And worse yet, what you did to your wife and son."

Up to this point, Luther said little. Did Belarus really know what happened to his wife and child? What Arminius remembered, he remembered well. Very well. He could still feel the movement of his unborn child in Thusnelda's womb and smell his wife's cooking. His shoulder still felt her arm as they lay asleep, side-by-side, and there was a residue of acknowledgement: he had always suspected that he was the cause for their disappearance. He finally spoke.

"I'm not alone, Count."

Belarus' contemptuous reply dripped with sarcasm. "What the hell is that supposed to mean?"

"God is with me. My family may be dead, but through God's Grace, I will see them again."

Belarus scoffed before he said with great satisfaction. "You will see them sooner than you think."

"Let me kill him," the young woman hissed.

"Now, now, dear. You are no match for Arminius. He is a professional. There are other ways. Go into the next room and bring out my prize."

Belarus laughed. "I have no doubt you have other tricks up your sleeve, Arminius. A direct assault from me? I don't think so. Not yet. Not when a flanking maneuver will do." After the young woman disappeared, Belarus continued. "You were saying something about your family being with your God. You couldn't be more right. I have waited for this moment with great anticipation."

Arminius watched the young woman return with another. He gasped. His legs buckled and he leaned against the door. Belarus didn't hide his immense pleasure at the reaction.

"Thusnelda...Thusnelda..." Arminius whispered. He watched his former wife move to the other side of Belarus. She was much younger than he remembered; it was obvious Belarus had returned her youth. She had sold her soul.

Thusnelda, his wife from two-thousand years ago looked directly into his eyes.

"Forgive me, my husband."

Belarus shook his head. "Ask him for nothing."

"My child...?" Arminius asked.

"You mean your son?" Belarus said, "Oh, your son. Yes. Well, I told

30

your lovely wife I would let him live if she agreed to become my bride. Personally, I think she got the better end of the deal."

"Forgive me, Arminius," she begged again.

"Besides," Belarus said, "I didn't need to kill your son. Your own people took care of that. They gave him to the Romans when they allowed your wife's capture. I don't think the Romans knew they were getting two-for-one."

Arminius had hoped against hope. Perhaps Belarus had other information. Arminius knew the history, but if Thusnelda was here, then perhaps his son...but that was not the case. In the end, he was unable to save either. The Romans turned his son into a gladiator and he died in the arena. That was a long time ago, as was the pain of the memory. Garner your emotions and stay focused, he told himself.

"Thusnelda, don't blame yourself," said Arminius.

Thusnelda looked at Arminius, her eyes regretful. "I did it for our son. Still, he died. Now, I can't stop. I need the Count's blood to live." She glanced at Dorothy. "I'm too weak-willed to kill myself and stop this nightmare."

Belarus cornered a small cigar shaped box on the desk. He opened it to reveal two flintlock hand weapons. He didn't remove them yet. "Enough family chitchat," he remarked. "As I already said, I knew you would eventually track me down, Arminius, and I saved your wife for such an occasion. She never truly bonded with me. Her love for you is strong. Now, I offer her to you. Come back to me, Arminius."

Was this a trap?

No. Belarus was sincere. He was offering Thusnelda; how could that be a trap?

Still, Arminius had no intention of turning his back on God. He observed Thusnelda shaking her head no.

She wanted to end this now.

He loved her dearly, or the thought of what she once was. If Belarus counted on that love to turn him, he had miscalculated. Arminius would release his wife from her bondage. He made his decision and began to formulate his strategy.

"Belarus, living forever has its inherent problems. You tend to find yourself living behind a mirror, watching the world pass by, seeing the pain of others and finding that pain reflected in your own soul. I'm sure Thusnelda understands that." He waited until she nodded before continuing. He pointed at the open box. "I don't suppose those are loaded?"

"Well, of course they are," responded Belarus. "They'd be useless otherwise."

Arminius coiled and sprang, removing a thin blade from a seam in his jacket. While shouting "I love you," he hurled the blade at Thusnelda.

The surgical sharpness entered her brain and killed her instantly.

She had to be his first target. His love for her demanded that.

She was free now, but the delay cost him. With skilled precision, he threw two balanced blades--both in the shape of a cross, at Belarus, aiming for his chest and head. The time it had taken him used to kill his wife gave Belarus time to grab the rejuvenated woman and offer her as a shield. She screamed and then fell to the floor dead, the top of her head nearly sliced off.

Arminius engaged the knife in his left sleeve. Secured to each wrist was a nine-inch blade, but he didn't stop there. He struck both blades together. Sparks preceded the hidden, thin blades that sprang open from each master blade to form a cross. He pointed both crosses at the Count and shouted: "It's time to die, Belarus!"

Belarus screamed. He withdrew the flintlock weapons and fired at Arminius. Both crosses on Arminius' wrist shattered from the impact of the conical projectiles. Still, the power of the crucifix resonated in Belarus' dark soul, and he had to use the desk for support. Both men stood facing each other, neither defenseless, and both waiting for the other to make the next move.

Arminius felt Dorothy weakly clawing at his ankles. He brought a foot down and crushed her skull. Better to put her out of misery. Besides, he didn't need the distraction.

"That wasn't nice," Belarus said, still gasping. "I was rather enjoying her suffering." He had the look of a man of hate, nothing more or less, simple loathing for an old friend. He glanced about the room. "Seems you've killed everything but me."

Plan B Arminius told himself. He knew bullets wouldn't kill a dark servant of hell, a .45 round impact would slow Belarus—maybe for long enough for him to think of something else. He pulled two automatics from the inside of his jacket and fired eight rounds from each clip—silver bullets that would kill a werewolf—into Belarus. Each bullet met its mark. The force of their impact sent Belarus over his desk and into the fireplace behind it.

Arminius wasted no time. He ran over to the ornate bookcase and slammed his elbow down on one of the shelves. The wood splintered while urns shattered on the rocky floor. Ripping off one of the longer splinters, he now held a stake. He barely made a move toward the fireplace before Belarus flew over the desk, his tattered suit smoking, hell's rage in his eyes, razor talons on his fingertips, mouth open wide exposing barbed thorns of death. "I'LL KILL YOU!"

Belarus was quick. Unearthly quick. There was no way Arminius could properly position the stake. He managed to slam the pointed end into Belarus' shoulder. Both men crashed to the floor with Belarus sliding until he slammed into the broken bookcase.

Arminius made a dash for the room from which Thusnelda had entered. As he suspected, the room opened to stairs, no doubt providing access to the upper levels of Erdely Castle. As he bounded up two steps at a time, other exits appeared on his right and left, likely leading to secret passages in this labyrinth of corridors. Any of the exits with doors, he opened. Let Belarus figure out which one he took.

He heard a menacing roar behind.

The next phase of his plan was to mingle with the guests above. He couldn't afford to expose his real motive to the group and wouldn't involve the others from the Paranormal Association group. This was his fight. It had been that way for the past two thousand years. No one could help him now, no one, as history proved, ever believed him when he explained his purpose in life: hunting evil. If not for God, he would be alone.

He was breathing heavily when he made it to the top. A latch on the inside swung a bookcase open and he was in a library.

A familiar voice spoke.

He searched for the source.

"Lord Erdely was a man of impeccable tastes. These paintings—"

Arminius turned a corner to meet Jennifer Brooks—the tour guide—leading a small group toward a hall adorned with paintings, each painting having above its frame a small light shining like a spotlight. Five of the paintings were of Romanian Kings, starting with Colonel Alexandru Ioan Cuza and ending with Carol II. Jennifer looked up to meet Arminius' wide-open eyes.

"—Mr. Hudson! Where have you been? You look like you've seen a monster. And your clothes—"

Arminius slowed his breathing. If only she knew.

"—where's your friend? Ms. McNally?"

"She picked up a crushing headache."

A boom of lightening seemed to crush the roof above them. The pane glass windows in that part of the castle cast moving patterns. In that light, Arminius saw the upside down crucifix at the bottom of the Grand Staircase next to a suit of armor. An upside down crucifix would have no affect on vampires, but he had an idea.

33

"That's too bad," Jennifer said. "I hope she feels better soon."

"So do I, Ms. Brooks. So do I. Now if you don't mind, I think I'll go find a place to dry."

"A good idea," her smile broadened, "for all of us to always listen to the tour guide. Maybe then we won't be soaked." She led the group down the hall and past the paintings. As soon as she was out of sight, Arminius dashed down the staircase.

The huge crucifix hung in a recessed wall niche. Three small metal prongs attached it from behind. Arminius grasped its horizontal axis and pulled.

It didn't budge. He needed leverage.

"Arminius...Arminius." The voice was from up the stairs. Belarus was there. "It's time to die, Arminius."

Arminius pulled as if his life depended on it—and it did. "Budge, damn you! Budge!" The crucifix remained firmly attached. Using the wall as leverage, he planted both feet against it and grasped the upper vertical axis this time. He yanked with all he had, straining and grunting.

"What are you doing?" The fat British man appeared from the darkness. Apparently, he had detached himself from the paranormal tour and remained downstairs. He stood next to the suit of armor and seemed to be debating what he would do next. It was obvious he was aghast at Arminius's behavior. Who wouldn't be? Arminius was trying to destroy a precious artifact and any decent fellow would have no part of it. "Now see here...a common thief?"

There was no way to reach the paranormal group now. A low growl followed by the sound of running footsteps and then the flutter of cloth in air told Arminius that Belarus had launched himself. There wasn't much time. Only seconds.

"GET OUT!" Arminius snapped at the Brit.

He glanced up the stairs. Belarus was almost on top of him now. There wasn't a second to waste. The cross bent parallel to the floor instead of breaking away. At that moment, Arminius executed a somersault by propelling himself from the wall.

Belarus crashed down, hurling the British man aside and into the suit of armor. The heavy metal shell came smashing down and pinned the fat man.

Like Arminius, the appearance of the Brit had surprised Belarus and threw him off stride.

That hesitation gave Arminius all the advantage he needed. As he flipped in the air, he planted both feet on Belarus' back and kicked, sending him into the exposed point of the bent cross.

Belarus was unable to stop his forward motion and impaled himself onto the crucifix. Arminius rolled onto his shoulder and sprang to his feet.

Belarus screamed in terrified horror as he faced his final embrace with the cross. The ravages of age tore at his body. The skin on his arms and face peeled off as if under an invisible knife. His neck turned blue-black like a big bruise and his fingertips swelled like ten individual water balloons—until each exploded.

The British man made his own chorus of terrified sounds; his mouth opened so wide in horror that it was easy to see his oscillating tongue dance in chorus with screams that rumbled from deep inside his throat—screams of dread. Dread that his world of absolutes had been shattered. Dread that something undead was decomposing before his eyes. Perhaps dread that Arminius would make him the next victim of this played out horror.

As if in stereo, Brit and Belarus shrieked, each pinned against his wish, both watching a world crash before his eyes. Belarus' face collapsed into itself, eye sockets—colored shadow dark—sucked in white ovals that stared in terror at the cross. His neck became brittle, unable to support his smoldering head, a thin film of fire spreading from his face to his torso. The skin around his neck tore. His head toppled backwards, still connected by a single flap of mummified skin. The head hung like that for what seemed an eternity. Sunken eyes stared at Arminius, and then the darkened skull ripped from the attached flesh and crashed to the floor, exploding into powder like a fragile urn, sending a dirty, white film onto the terror ravished Brit like a blanket of dust, turning his fat round face into a chalk colored moon. Shocked, the Brit simply went silent, his eyes wide and round.

Arminius stepped back and looked up.

Above the crucifix hung a grossly gigantic picture of Vlad the Impaler, King of Romania. Strike another one up for the good guys. He lowered his eyes and studied the Brit. The opportunity was too good to pass up.

"Explain that."

* * * *

Arminius sat in a small coffee shop situated along Route 66 in Oklahoma. From his pocket, he pulled out a recent news article from the Tulsa Tribune. The author wrote of missing babies—Mexican babies. Local authorities suspected a satanic cult. Staring past the article, Arminius contemplated his next move.

"Can I get you another cup of coffee?" The server was of Indian descent and had the noble face of a full blood.

"No thanks...I've had enough." He laid a five on the table and told her to keep the change.

"Thanks," she said. "Where'ya heading?"

He stood, stuffing the article in his shirt pocket. He kicked an old, crumpled receipt from his path with cowboy boots and then put on a cowboy hat. His pants were dusty, and the old Chevy pickup waiting for him outside was worn and rusty.

"Mexico," he said, and then left.

AUTHOR'S BIO:

William Koonce is a writer of Dark Christian Fiction, grateful for a loving God and a loving wife. Some of his work can found at www.wildkite.com.

THE MARK
By
Eric Keith

The first sighting came the moment after Charlie Alexander stepped into Erdely Castle.

Charlie and Helen were the first to enter.

Charlie was struck at once by the imposing paintings glaring at him accusingly from high on the oak walls. The subject, stern-featured like a judge, was presumably Lord Erdely. In one painting he wore a ruffled shirt and astrakhan, a Russian-style cap made of curly wool. In another, he sported a white tunic and, on his head, something resembling a red fez. A third painting showed him in what looked like a mauve smoking jacket and matching nightcap. Strange... that in each picture his...

A muffled cry and hollow thud spun Charlie and Helen sharply around. Mrs. Harris lay on the floor behind them, face down, just beyond the threshold step, only inches from the castle's front entrance. The young, handsome Dr. Franklin raced to her aid.

On the bus ride here, Helen had sat between Franklin and Charlie. Charlie had been displeased with the seating arrangement; but fortunately, Dr. Franklin did not seem to pay Helen any attention, much to Charlie's relief. Still, Charlie and Helen uttered not a word during the entire bus ride.

Dr. Franklin examined Mrs. Harris. "She's uninjured," he pronounced. "There's a step here at the front door; she didn't see it. It's not visible from outside. How treacherous: it's a miracle everyone entering the castle doesn't get hurt."

While the guests were distracted by Mrs. Harris's fall, Charlie turned in response to a sound across the large salon: someone had entered the room.

It was a tall man in lavender servant's livery, roughly Charlie's age of fifty-five. The man stopped abruptly, staring at Charlie as if recognizing him.

Strangely, something seemed familiar about the servant, as well, though Charlie could swear he had never seen him before. Charlie could not read the expression in the intruder's face: surprise, shock, fear?

Fear it must have been, for he turned to flee, exposing, as he did, his right cheek to Charlie's view. The entire right side of the servant's face was horribly deformed, pink and puckered... burned, Charlie realized.

"Wait!" Charlie called, determined to learn who he was.

But it was too late: the intruder had vanished. Charlie tried to pursue, following him around two corners. The stranger entered a room at the far side of a dead-end hallway. In a daze, Charlie crossed the eerie corridor, as if he had done so dozens of times in some long-forgotten dream, vaguely afraid of what he might find if he followed his prey through the door at the far end. After all, the servant had seemed less to be fleeing than leading Charlie on...

Puzzled by his strange apprehension, Charlie pushed open the door to a bedroom. A four-post bed dominated the room. Old, grubby brown wallpaper was peeling at the edges. Ugly green curtains covered the window...

And nothing more. No stranger huddled inside. The room was empty.

The window, Charlie thought: *he had to have climbed out the window.* Charlie crossed the room and pushed aside the curtain, to discover the window latched from within.

Impossible: the door and window were the only ways out of the room. The stranger could not have left through the window and re-latched it from outside the castle. Nor had he come back out through the door: Charlie would have seen him. So he had to still be here. Hiding. Charlie shot a glance around the room. No closet. Only one place to hide: under the bed.

Slowly Charlie went down on all fours. With two fingers he pinched the corner of the bedspread. Trying not to tremble, he pried it up and opened his eyes.

No one.

Maybe he had the wrong room... No, he had clearly seen the stranger duck into this room. He had not imagined it.

Maybe he had imagined the stranger...

"I see you've found a room, Mr. Alexander."

Charlie turned. Miss Brooks, their tour guide, and a few of the other guests stood in the doorway. Bewildered by Charlie's sudden, unexplained flight from the salon, some of the guests had come looking for him.

"We know we're staying in the castle for at least one night," Miss Brooks continued. "We're not going anywhere in this storm. And since you seem to have chosen your room already, you can have this one."

"Did any of you see him?" Charlie cried.

Helen appeared from behind Miss Brooks. "See who?" she asked.

"The man in the salon: a servant, with a burned face."

"There *are* no servants here," Miss Brooks said. "The Paranormal Association has a staff of workers that keep up the castle; but they do so strictly in-between tours."

"But I saw him... dressed in servant's livery... didn't anyone see him?"

No one else had.

"He came in here," Charlie insisted.

Professor Langer stepped into the room and looked around. "Then where is he?"

"Out the window," Miss Brooks suggested.

"It's locked," Charlie said.

"Under the bed."

"I checked."

"Are you saying he just disappeared?" Helen asked.

"Maybe it was a ghost," that mean man, Mr. Willows, teased.

"Actually," said Miss Brooks, "Erdely Castle *is* said to be haunted." Her tone was light, with a dismissive giggle, yet Charlie sensed an undertone of gravity.

"Maybe Mr. Alexander has encountered the castle ghost," suggested that slender teenaged girl–what was her name?–the one dressed all in black... Samantha.

"Then why has it revealed itself only to him?" Professor Langer wondered aloud.

When the others departed to receive their room assignments, Charlie, alone now, looked once more around the room. He wondered why he felt so uncomfortable here. Maybe it was the hideous green curtains that looked at least forty years old. In a fit of resolution, Charlie hastened to the window and tore down the curtains, tossing them under the bed.

That was when he noticed the wallpaper seam that had begun to peel from the wall, exposing a dark spot behind it.

Crawling over the bed, Charlie folded back the wallpaper: only a fraction of an inch, at first, but then more. The entire exposed area was black. He rubbed his finger on the wall, then examined his blackened finger.

On every wall, Charlie widened breaches in the seams, uncovering the same black underbelly.

All four walls were charred.

* * * *

Helen, in her white blouse buttoned up to the black choker around her neck and tight blue skirt hiding her knees, stood before the fireplace mantle, to the left of the fire, examining the curios on the mantle shelf.

"A nice-looking girl," Dr. Franklin muttered to Charlie, staring at the fireplace.

Even a fire cannot rout the chill from a seventeenth-century castle during a thunderstorm; yet suddenly Charlie felt very hot. He hazarded a glance at Dr. Franklin, and then realized: the doctor was looking to the right of the fire, at Miss Brooks. Charlie unclenched his white-knuckled fists and relaxed.

An explosion of thunder made everyone jump. The guests had reassembled in the salon as if to brace together against the violence of the storm. Charlie did not mind the storm: it was during a thunderstorm that he had met Helen Grace. Charlie couldn't even remember when it was she had first appeared at his doorstep: it seemed like ages ago. She lived in an apartment three floors above his, she said, and the storm had knocked out her electricity: she'd asked to borrow candles.

How young and innocent she had looked, a girl of twenty-five with a pink ribbon in her hair, like the one she wore now. From that moment he knew they would be friends, despite their age difference; even now he felt so comfortable with her, as if he had known her, not for years, but for decades. She seemed to know him so well: not once, for instance, had she ever worn anything green, though Charlie had never told her he detested the color.

Miss Brooks had apparently noticed the anxiety the storm's fury had sown in some of the guests. A consummate tour guide, she used distraction to put them at ease.

"In the early seventeenth century, Erdely Castle was leveled by a storm." Hardly reassuring, Charlie thought. "But even then, miraculously, there were no casualties."

"And the paintings–of Lord Erdely, I presume–appear to have been spared, as well," Professor Langer observed.

"The storm predated Lord Erdely's residency," Miss Brooks explained. "In fact, it was Lord Erdely who had the castle rebuilt–and renamed."

Miss Brooks had told them all about Lord Erdely's interest in black magic and opposition to the Church; how he had reportedly sealed his servants' ears before sending them on errands, to keep them from hearing words spoken to them outside the castle.

"Those portraits are creepy," said the black-clad Samantha.

"Now Samantha," warned her mother.

"No—she's right," said Charlie. "There's something very peculiar about those paintings."

Miss Brooks welcomed the change of subject. "To what are you referring, Mr. Alexander?"

"Well, all of the portraits were painted indoors. Look, in this one you can see the banquet hall table behind Lord Erdely. And in that one, in the background, you can look out the window to the trees in front of the castle. Yet in all of the paintings, Lord Erdely is wearing a hat or some kind of head covering... indoors."

"No one has ever pointed that out before, Mr. Alexander," said Miss Brooks enthusiastically. "That's most interesting."

"Maybe he was bald," Samantha said.

"Lord Erdely had raven-black hair," Miss Brooks countered.

"It's not just his head that's covered," Dr. Franklin pointed out. "He has chosen headgear that covers his <u>forehead</u>, as well."

"How very strange," Helen agreed.

A second peal of thunder sent a shudder through the room. Even Charlie flinched at the crash of rain laying siege to the castle walls. In his mind he felt it drench his clothes and chill his flesh, as it had thirty years ago, a homeless immigrant in Philadelphia. Had he not met Father Clemens in the shelter, he might still be living on the street. It was Father Clemens who had gotten him a job as janitor in that textile plant. Eventually Charlie was able to afford an apartment in an old brownstone building downtown. So long ago: he could not even remember a life before that.

The rain's amplifying drumbeat was echoed by a crescendo of anxiety in the guests, taxing the social skills of their hostess.

"Who's hungry?" asked Miss Brooks. "I'll go check on our provisions while everyone prepares for lunch. We'll all feel a lot better once we've eaten."

The moment Charlie opened his bedroom door, he knew something was wrong. What? Everything was as it had been...

Yes... that was the problem. *Some*thing should not have been the same. With a gasp Charlie realized what it was.

The curtains. The horrid green curtains he had tossed under the bed. They were back on the window.

What was going on?

But there was something even more disturbing. Something that didn't belong. He could sense it before he could see it. A slight movement drew his eyes upward.

Dangling from the ceiling, the body of—he couldn't tell if it was a woman or a man—hung by a rope around the neck.

Charlie could not stifle a scream—of horror more than fear. Blindly he fled from the room, down the hallway. Before his moist eyes could focus, he felt himself collide with someone.

Dr. Franklin.

"Whoa, Charlie, what's wrong? You look like you've seen a ghost."

"In my room..." Charlie stammered. "A body... strangled."

"What are you talking about?"

"Come look..." Heavy panting made Charlie hard to understand. "...in my room..."

"Take it easy. You want me to look in your room?" Charlie nodded. "All right. Let's take a look."

Even with the protection of Dr. Franklin, Charlie was afraid to return. He let the doctor lead the way.

"All right," Dr. Franklin said. "What am I looking for?"

It was impossible. Dr. Franklin stood in the doorway. He should have been staring right at it.

"Hanging from the ceiling," Charlie muttered as he stepped out from behind the doctor.

What in the world...

"I don't see anything hanging from the ceiling," the doctor protested.

It was gone.

"But it was here," Charlie insisted. "I saw it."

"Looks like you're the victim of a cruel hoax," Dr. Franklin said. "Your 'body' seems to have left the room while you were in the hallway."

"How did it get out?"

The doctor pointed. "Window's the only way out."

Charlie hastened to the curtains and drew them aside. The window was latched.

"How did it relock the window from the outside?"

For the first time Dr. Franklin looked grave. "He couldn't have." The doctor had lowered his voice as he glanced around the room. "Which means he's still here." Quietly he approached the bed, dropped to his knees, and searched beneath it. "Only he's not," he said, rising. "Yet the only other way out is the door—and I was in the hallway facing your room. I would have seen him if he had come out."

"Not if he was imaginary," came a voice from behind. Both men turned: Mr. Willows stood in the doorway. "Maybe our friend Mr. Alexander is delusional."

Behind Mr. Willows Helen appeared, looking anxious. "Are you all right, Charlie?" she cried. "I heard a scream."

"I'm fine," Charlie said.

"Are you?" asked Mr. Willows. "Or are you suffering from some kind of nervous breakdown?"

"It's just shock," Dr. Franklin explained. "From his encounter this morning."

"With the servant with the burned face? A man who magically disappeared from this very room, leaving the window locked and the door watched by Charlie himself? What was it, Charlie, the castle ghost?" Mr. Willows' eyes narrowed. "Or is that what we're supposed to think? How do we know you haven't been planted here to scare us, to make the more feebleminded of us think the castle is haunted? After all, you're not even really one of the guests."

Mr. Willows was right. Three days ago, Helen Grace had received a telegram from Romania: it appeared Helen had an aunt living in this country—until last week, when the aunt passed away, leaving behind a small bequest to her only living relative, Helen. Helen was invited to travel to Romania to settle the estate.

"Why don't you come with me?" Helen had asked Charlie. "It'll be fun."

"But that would take most of my savings—"

"Don't worry about that. We'll just reimburse you from my aunt's bequest."

"I don't know, Helen—"

"Come on. I'll be in a foreign country. You can protect me."

She finally prevailed upon him. Her aunt's lawyer had already booked her a room at the Hotel Cornifu, and Helen offered to reserve one for Charlie by phone.

But when they arrived at the hotel, no record of Charlie's reservation could be found. To make matters worse, the hotel was full.

"But it's not our fault you lost the reservation," Helen cried. "You *have* to find him a room."

The desk clerk ignored her.

"Can't you find *something?*" Charlie asked meekly.

The clerk searched his computer. "Ah, you're in luck. Mr. Higgins, in Room 208, was stricken by malaria and rushed to the hospital last night. He'll be there for a few days: I could give you his room—for a night or two, at least."

It was in Room 208 that Charlie found Mr. Higgins's invitation to the Erdely Castle tour.

"Sounds like fun," Helen said. "My meeting with the lawyer is not for two days; and the tour's tomorrow. Let's go—can we, Charlie?"

"We don't have invitations."

"We have this."

"It's not in my name."

"Tell them Mr. Higgins got sick, and you're his cousin. I'll go as your guest."

"You mean, lie?"

"Mr. Higgins really did get sick."

"I'm not his cousin."

"How do you know? Maybe you *are* related. Come on, Charlie. *He* can't go. Don't let the invitation go to waste."

Charlie could never say no to Helen. Her plan worked: no one questioned Charlie's relation to Mr. Higgins.

Dr. Franklin was defending Charlie to Mr. Willows. "If Charlie is here to scare us," he said, "I don't think it's working. He looks more frightened than any of us."

"If he's not a plant," Mr. Willows said dryly, "then he must have really seen a ghost. What other explanation is there?"

"Yes..." Dr. Franklin suddenly looked preoccupied. "What other...?"

"It's not funny," Helen cried. "Can't you see there's something strange going on here?"

"More than strange," Charlie said. "It could be dangerous."

"What...?" exclaimed Mr. Willows. "What are you talking about?" He turned from Charlie to Dr. Franklin with bewildered appeal.

But the doctor was paying no attention. Instead, he scurried from the room into the hallway, to which other curious guests had begun to gravitate. Outside Charlie's room, the doctor studied the dead-end corridor, with particular interest in the wall that sealed off the hallway just past Charlie's bedroom door. If the guests had concerns over Charlie's mental well-being, they now transferred them to Dr. Franklin as they watched him rap his knuckles against various sections of wall, listening intently to the echoes that answered each knock.

With puckered brow the doctor stepped back, scrutinizing the wall. He seemed to be admiring the sole painting hung there, a portrait of Lord Erdely in a white frock and beige stocking cap concealing his forehead. A strange place for a painting, Charlie thought.

Dr. Franklin seemed to echo this opinion, as he, with a sudden sharp intake of breath, approached the portrait and removed it from the wall. Setting it on the floor, he studied the wall, clothed now only with the hook from which the portrait had hung. Tentatively the doctor stretched forth his hand to touch the hook. With sudden resolution, his fingers enfolded it and tugged it downward.

A loud click preceded a noise like stone rolling on stone. Charlie noticed a small gap on both sides of the hook, from ceiling to floor: a section of wall had pivoted on its axis.

"A secret passage!" Helen exclaimed.

Dr. Franklin put his shoulder to the left side of the wall, but the stone partition was too heavy to budge. Several of the stupefied onlookers added their weight, and the wall swiveled clockwise to reveal a large chamber.

"A hidden room."

Dr. Franklin stepped into the room and flicked on the light switch. Filing cabinets and shelves with beakers and what looked like medical equipment lined the walls. In the center of the room sat a long silver table, beside which an aluminum cart on wheels supported a metal box with dials and two wires sprouting from the sides.

"What is this place?" asked Mr. Willows.

He was not the only one who so wondered. By now many of the guests had been attracted by the commotion and migrated to its source.

"How did you know this room was here?" Helen asked Dr. Franklin.

But the doctor was absorbed in his study of the metal box beside the silver table. He held the two black wires, studying the disk-like growths at their tips.

"Electrodes," he muttered.

"What *is* this thing?" Professor Langer asked.

Dr. Franklin's eyes grew dark. "If I'm not mistaken, it's an electroshock machine."

"What is an electroshock machine doing in a seventeenth century castle?" asked the teenager, Samantha.

"That's what *I'm* wondering." Dr. Franklin looked around. "Maybe the answer is somewhere in this room."

On cue, everyone began searching the chamber. But the file cabinets were empty, and the drawers and shelves yielded no clue.

"Any records of what went on here have been hidden," Professor Langer observed. "Or destroyed."

It was Charlie who noticed the darker stone near the bottom of the north wall.

Trancelike he approached it, placing his hand on the blemished square with a tentative push. The stones above it receded as the panel hidden beneath them recessed into the wall and disappeared behind the stones above. In their place a dark alcove remained.

"What the—" Mr. Willows began.

"What is it?" Helen asked.

"I don't know," Charlie muttered.

Watching Charlie with a puzzled expression, Dr. Franklin drew near, kneeling beside him to examine the stone Charlie had pressed.

"Darker than its neighbors," the doctor observed. "You are not the first person to touch this stone, Charlie: it's been pushed often enough before. That's what darkened it. Obviously the former occupants of this castle knew about this secret compartment, and enjoyed opening it."

"The question is," Professor Langer said, "what was in it?"

"We'll probably never know," the doctor replied. "Whoever amused himself by playing with the secret nook undoubtedly discovered its contents long ago."

Nonetheless Dr. Franklin reached into the alcove, and, surprisingly, withdrew something from it. The room's other occupants crowded around to see what he had found.

It was a small sheathe of papers.

Dr. Franklin examined the papers, one by one. They were all drawings: drawings of the same thing, sketched from different angles, in different sizes, with different shadings; but all fundamentally the same:

T

"The letter 'T,'" Helen said.

"What is it?" asked Samantha.

"You said this compartment had been opened repeatedly," Mr. Willows objected, "and the contents undoubtedly found and removed." He pointed to the drawings. "So what are these doing here?"

Dr. Franklin shook his head. "It seems unlikely they were overlooked."

"Perhaps the people who found them were *afraid* to remove them," Professor Langer suggested.

"Afraid?" asked Helen. "Why?"

But Professor Langer maintained a stubborn silence. His small eyes and wrinkled forehead reflected a grave and troubled spirit.

"Why would anyone be afraid of the letter 'T'?" asked Samantha.

"It's not a 'T,'" replied Professor Langer. The others regarded him with bewildered expressions. "I'm a professor of religion," Langer explained. "My expertise is with primitive religions, which gives me some knowledge of primitive culture and various languages. I even know some Romanian," he boasted. He held up the drawings. "The symbol on these drawings—a Tau Cross, it's called—goes back to the beginning of recorded history. It was a mystic symbol used by the Babylonians and ancient Egyptians. It was placed on the foreheads of people initiated into the ancient mysteries during baptism. It was considered a sacred symbol."

"These drawings don't look like they were made by ancient Babylonians," observed Dr. Franklin.

"No," agreed Professor Langer. "But look how brown and dried-out the paper appears. These were made hundreds of years ago."

"By who?" Samantha asked.

"My guess? By Lord Erdely himself."

"But why would he be interested in some ancient Babylonian symbol?"

"*I* may be able to answer that." Everyone turned: Miss Brooks had silently slipped into the secret chamber. "Lord Erdely was deeply interested in the black arts. If this—what did you call it, a Tau Cross?—was used by ancient mystery cults, they probably believed it had some kind of mystic power. And *that* would be of interest to Lord Erdely."

"What kind of power are we talking about?" Dr. Franklin asked Professor Langer.

The professor looked grim.

"No one knows."

* * * *

Lunch proved uneventful–for everyone but Charlie. The water pitchers and butter trays had been placed on the large oak dining table before it was realized that more tables would be needed. Two side tables were added, each borrowing a pitcher and butter tray from the main table. Charlie and Helen were seated at a small table with Mr. Willows and two other guests Charlie did not know. As Mr. Willows reached for the empty water pitcher later in the meal, Helen dropped her fork on the floor.

"We're out of water," Mr. Willows complained.

"And I need a new fork," Helen added irritably.

Charlie stood up. "Don't worry, I'll get it."

Passing the main table, Charlie heard Mr. Willows call out, "Hey, where are you—" as Charlie stepped into the kitchen to find a fork.

Charlie stopped abruptly. Bent over an open drawer, his back to Charlie, stood a servant in purple livery. But Miss Brooks had said that no servants... Hearing Charlie's entrance, the servant turned his head.

The right side of his face was burned.

It was he: the man Charlie had seen this morning in the salon. The one no one else had seen. The one who had disappeared inexplicably from Charlie's room.

The servant did not seem surprised to see Charlie. In fact, a malignant smile coiled like a snake on his lips. Yet, though clearly unafraid, the servant retreated from the kitchen through a side door as Charlie stood paralyzed.

Snap out of it, Charlie told himself. Everyone thought he was imagining this servant; Charlie, himself, was not even sure. He had to find out.

Charlie dashed out of the kitchen's side door on time to see his quarry disappear down one of the castle's labyrinthine corridors. Though Charlie ran, somehow his prey managed to always stay one corridor ahead. But that was about to change.

The last hallway was a dead end. No doors or windows on either side. The servant was trapped.

Except for one thing... when Charlie got there, the servant was gone.

The hallway was empty.

How was that possible? Charlie had seen him turn down this corridor: there was no mistake about that. So where had he gone? Real people don't just vanish like that.

Did that mean he wasn't real? Was everyone right: was he just a figment of Charlie's imagination?

Or was he something else? Charlie knew Mr. Willows had only been teasing; but could the old man have been right: had Charlie been chasing a ghost? A ghost that could pass through walls? A ghost only Charlie could see?

But why was it showing itself only to Charlie?

"What happened?"

Charlie turned: it was Helen.

"I was worried about you," she said. "Why did you disappear like that?"

Charlie told her about the ghost, or whatever it was.

Helen's eyes darkened. "What does it want with you?"

"I don't know."

"So what are you going to do?"

But Charlie didn't answer: his eye had been caught by a glint from the floor at the end of the hallway. Cautiously he approached, then stooped to pick up an object lying next to the wall.

A gold locket. With a photograph inside.

"What is it?" Helen asked.

But Charlie could not bring himself to answer. He merely held out the locket for her to see.

"Me," Helen gasped.

It was indeed a photograph of Helen Grace, taken recently, it seemed.

"What's it doing here, inside this castle?" she asked. "How did someone get a photograph of me? No one knew I'd be coming." She shivered. "Charlie, I'm scared." Fitfully she adjusted the pink ribbon in her hair.

Charlie had to say something to comfort her. "I'm sure there's a logical explanation for this."

His reassurance seemed to have a calming effect, for Helen vouchsafed him a tiny smile. "Well, whoever this belongs to doesn't hold me in much esteem: look at the locket. It's all tarnished. The least the owner could have done was to buy a new locket for the picture."

Even when frightened, Helen tried to put on a cheerful disposition. Though she herself was upset, she did not want to worry Charlie: always thinking of others, even when she was the one in need. No wonder he felt about her as he did. He could not even remember a time before she came into his life.

Could he ever confide those feelings in her? Something warned Charlie against it. Whether it was the thirty years that separated them, or something else, Charlie knew somehow she would not mirror his feelings, were he to hold them up to her. Better not to jeopardize the friendship they *did* have.

Thumping footsteps announced the sudden arrival of Dr. Franklin in the hallway.

"So there you are," he told Charlie. "I've been looking all over for you. You just disappeared, and some of us were starting to worry. Why did you run off?"

Charlie was not about to tell him of the man, or specter, he had been chasing, who had disappeared mysteriously from this very corridor. Enough of the guests already thought Charlie was imagining the elusive spirit–or making him up to scare them; he didn't need to add fuel to the fire.

"It's the thunder," Charlie said. "It was so loud. I suppose I was afraid of another storm, like the one that destroyed the castle four hundred years ago. I figured I'd be safer in my room... but I got lost..."

Would Dr. Franklin believe him? Charlie studied the doctor's face; but the doctor no longer seemed to be listening.

"Of course..." he muttered. "That's it." He patted Charlie's shoulder. "Charlie, you're a genius."

Charlie stood slack-jawed as Dr. Franklin scampered off; but the towline of curiosity tugged Charlie in the doctor's wake, with Helen as tireless shadow close behind.

The oak staircase was their first and final port of call. Charlie watched in bewilderment as Dr. Franklin conducted a fretful examination of the area around–and beneath–the staircase. He virtually threw himself against the wall under the stairs, pressing every square inch with hands, arms, even knees. Finally his efforts were rewarded with a faint click.

Dr. Franklin pivoted the secret door on its axis and stepped inside. Cautiously Charlie and Helen followed him into the dark. But it was not a room that greeted them beyond the hidden panel: instead, they descended a murky, narrow staircase. A handful of guests, drawn from the dining room by the sounds of the search, followed close behind.

At the foot of the stairs, Dr. Franklin called out, "Matches, anyone?"

Someone behind Charlie handed him a book of matches, which he passed along to Dr. Franklin. Hiss and spark, smell of sulfur, and the gloom was beaten back by the kindling torch Dr. Franklin had found on the wall.

The receding curtain of dark exposed stone walls, oak desks, and metal filing cabinets.

"Miss Brooks told us that a storm leveled the castle centuries ago," the doctor explained, "yet there were no casualties. I wondered how that could be... until I realized that the survivors must have taken refuge in some kind of cellar." The doctor swept a hand across the chamber. "This is that cellar."

"And what is it you expect to find here?" Charlie asked.

"Answers, I hope."

Dr. Franklin began sifting through filing cabinets and desk drawers, poring over documents with the zeal of a child unearthing pirates' treasure.

The weariness that had been pursuing Charlie's spirits finally caught up. Adding its weight to Charlie's disinterest in historical color, it seized his limbs with leaden numbness. He needed to rest a while in his own room.

But rest was the one thing he did not find there.

What he *did* find, upon returning to his room, froze him in his tracks not far beyond the threshold. In paralyzed stillness Charlie gaped at the wall to his left. There, in leprous white paint rising from the grave of a dirty brown wall, a life-sized image greeted Charlie's mute entrance into the room:

T

It was the—what had Professor Langer called it?—the Tau Cross, the ancient mystic symbol. Someone had painted it on the wall. But why? Why Charlie's room?

And how? Charlie had locked both door and window before leaving the room. He had to unlock the door with his key just now; and the window was still latched. How could anyone have gotten into the room? He'd have to be a...

... ghost...

"Redecorating?" came a voice from behind.

Charlie turned: Professor Langer stared at the Tau Cross on the wall.

"I didn't paint that."

"Then who did?"

Charlie's shoulders slumped helplessly.

"We have to notify someone," the professor said. "Something's going on here, although I'm damned if I know what it is. But Miss Brooks knows more about this place than anyone; and she's in charge. I think she needs to see this."

By now lunch was long past; Miss Brooks could be anywhere. They would have to seek her out.

A sound from one of the castle's "house of mirrors" corridors caught Charlie's ear and tugged his head around. As if it were Charlie's reflection in a glass, a second head peered around the corner behind him, echoing Charlie's gaze—a head he recognized.

Was it really there? No one else had seen the servant—or whatever it was—since their arrival at Erdely Castle. Charlie was afraid to draw the professor's attention to it: afraid that he, Charlie, might be the only one who saw it.

"What is it?"

Professor Langer was staring at him strangely. Of course he was: how could he have not noticed Charlie's odd behavior?

Charlie could not speak. He simply raised a mute finger and spun it behind them. The professor's eyes followed the finger.

The specter was gone.

"I don't see anything," Professor Langer said. He studied Charlie with uncomfortable intensity. "Did you see something?"

If he told the professor what he had seen, could Charlie doubt the professor's response? What could this be but a conspiracy to make

Charlie seem—or go—insane? Palsied with indecision, Charlie felt trapped, like a beast in a cage. What should he do? Faltering reason buckled beneath the flood of surging passion.

"I am not crazy!" Charlie exclaimed as he bolted off, blindly determined to make the hunter, imagined or real, his prey—and return with the trophy of proof.

The professor's vain cries could not keep pace with Charlie's zeal and fell behind as Charlie burst into the salon on time to see his liveried quarry bound up the stairs across the room. But why would a ghost flee one who could do it no possible harm? That is what Charlie intended to discover when he ran the spirit to ground.

The fugitive disappeared at the top of the stairs before Charlie reached the base. Charlie mounted in leaps, two steps at a time, past portraits of Lord Erdely, capped or hatted in each, that blurred and diffused in the heat of Charlie's resolve to lay hands upon the specter, if hands could indeed grasp it.

But Charlie was not to pass the topmost step. Was the fugitive really fleeing, or luring Charlie on... into a trap? It had turned right at the top of the stairs. Before Charlie's body could trim its course, a form materialized before his eyes: the apparition jumped out from the wall behind the right staircase banister.

Perhaps even more shocking than the sudden appearance of the spectral form only inches from his face was that, for the first time, it hissed forth words. Or sounds, at least; for Charlie was so stricken by shock (*Could ghosts speak? Or was this proof that the "ghost" was really a flesh-and-blood creature?*) that he could not process the unexpected utterings, beyond the crazed impression they sounded vaguely like the words, "Colonel Sanders" (*was* Charlie in fact losing his mind?).

But there was no time to ponder questions that flashed through his mind like streaks of lightning in a midnight sky. The startling manifestation of the large char-faced figure sent a convulsive spasm through Charlie's body, reflexively yanking him backwards at the stair top. The hand of death clutched his shoulders and, with gravity's grip, drew him to his doom.

A backward fall from this height would break his neck. As Charlie felt the back of his head slice through the infinite emptiness behind him, he thought only of Helen, and his regret that even if he lived, he'd be no closer to his heart's desire than he would be dead.

But what was this? The impact came sooner and softer than he had expected. His plunge was arrested, not by the black arms of death, but by some unknown (divine?) agency.

No. No angel had caught him mid-fall. Human hands wrapped around his chest.

"Careful," came a voice behind him. "If you race up the stairs like that, *your* ghost will be haunting this place."

Charlie recognized the voice: it was Dr. Franklin.

The doctor helped him down the stairs. "I was in the cellar," Franklin explained, "when I heard footsteps trampling on the staircase. I came out to see what the commotion was all about. Lucky for you I did."

Charlie tried to catch his breath. "How many sets of footsteps?"

"What?"

"How many sets of footsteps did you hear? One or two?"

"I couldn't tell. It was pretty muffled down there."

"What's in the cellar?" asked a new voice. Professor Langer had caught up with Charlie: not on time to see him fall, apparently, but soon enough to overhear his conversation with Dr. Franklin.

"The cellar is where someone chose to store documents," Dr. Franklin explained.

"Documents? What kind of documents?"

"I don't know. They're in some language I don't speak: Romanian, I assume. A group of us was exploring the cellar, but that's all we found. The others finally got bored and left."

"And you have no idea what those documents could be?"

"Well, I recognized a few of the Latin words: medical terms. Together with the electroshock machine we found, I would hazard a guess that at some time in the recent past, Erdely Castle functioned as a mental hospital."

"I can read some Romanian," Professor Langer revealed, "having studied the Romanian branch of the Eastern Orthodox Church. That's what I'm doing in this country, as a matter of fact: research on the church. Perhaps I can translate some of those documents you found."

Dr. Franklin led Professor Langer and Charlie down the hidden stairs to the cellar, where the professor studied several of the documents. At length he offered his analysis.

"You appear to be right, Dr. Franklin—that is, if my Romanian is not deceiving me. Erdely Castle *was* used as a lunatic asylum until thirty years ago, when a twenty-five-year-old male patient named Carol Sandu murdered a female patient of similar age named Ileana Anca: strangled her with the curtain sash from her own room. Apparently he was in love with her, but her affections belonged to a patient named Emilian. Carol decided that if he couldn't have Ileana, no one would.

"After the murder, perhaps in a fit of guilt and remorse, Carol set Ileana's room on fire, remaining inside himself. The fire was put out before it could spread to the rest of the castle--one advantage of stone walls--but not before Carol was presumably consumed by the flames: his body was never found. Naturally, the response to this tragedy was the immediate shutdown of the asylum."

His traumatic near-death experience on the stairs, Charlie decided, must have been what had seized his limbs with a weary dullness. He had to sit down and rest: but the cellar offered nothing even resembling a chair. At length Charlie slumped to the floor, his back propped against a wall. He tried to fight the wave of nausea and dizziness by focusing across the room.

Helen appeared in the doorway: how did she find them?

"What's everyone doing?" she asked as the room's occupants continued to examine documents.

"We've been digging up secrets," Charlie said dryly.

Dr. Franklin turned puzzled eyes on Charlie. "That's one way to put it, I suppose." His tone seemed patronizing, as if talking to a child.

Professor Langer was staring at Charlie strangely. "Are you all right, Charlie? You look pale."

"Charlie had a nasty experience on the stairs," Dr. Franklin explained. "A near-fatal one."

They would ask what had happened on the staircase. What would he tell them? That the apparition of the man no one else could see had jumped in front of him at the top of the stairs, seemingly from out of nowhere, startling Charlie and sending him headlong down the staircase? Charlie was becoming less afraid of the ghost–if that's what it was–than of the others' response to him having seen it.

Helen looked flustered. "Are you sure you're all right, Charlie?"

"I'm fine," he insisted.

"What happened on that staircase?" Dr. Franklin asked. "Did you lose your balance?"

"I don't know what happened."

"You know," the doctor said, "if it was a dizzy spell, or something like that, it could be indicative of a more serious problem." Dr. Franklin set down the papers he was holding and moved toward Charlie. "Perhaps I should take a look at you, just to be sure."

Reflexively Charlie recoiled, pressing with bent legs his back against the wall. He did not need a doctor poking and prodding.

"I told you, I'm fine."

The doctor stopped abruptly. "Did you hear that?"

Charlie had indeed. A loud clack had accompanied the pressure of Charlie's back against the wall.

"Charlie, stand up."

Puzzled by Dr. Franklin's request, Charlie nonetheless complied. The doctor examined the section of wall Charlie had just vacated. A seam had been exposed.

"Charlie, I think you just discovered a secret door."

The doctor dug his fingers into the newly exposed crevice, prying the left edge of a concealed panel from the wall. The stone door turned on its hinges.

"A hidden room," Helen muttered.

Dr. Franklin lit the torch he found in the musty secret chamber, and the others followed him inside. A private office: mahogany desk. Velvet-backed chairs. A carpet of indeterminate color lay on the stone floor.

Hungrily the explorers swarmed the desk, pillaging its drawers. But they had not been expecting what they found.

Dozens of drawings, browned and yellowed with age: most of them accompanied by words, written in a language even Professor Langer could not identify.

"They appear to be some kind of spells," he guessed.

"Makes sense," Dr. Franklin agreed. "Miss Brooks told us that Lord Erdely was passionately interested in the occult."

"Black magic spells?" Helen asked.

"But what about the drawings?"

For it was the drawings that disturbed the guests: dozens of drawings of what Professor Langer had called the "Tau Cross".

The most disturbing discovery was what they found in the bottom drawer.

"Lord Erdely," Charlie said.

They were looking at sketches of a human head, whose features did indeed resemble those of the man in the portraits upstairs. Most troubling, however, was not that someone had sketched Lord Erdely's face; it was what the artist had drawn on Erdely's forehead.

"The Tau Cross."

In sketch after sketch, the artist had drawn the Tau Cross on Lord Erdely's forehead, and had taken the trouble to paint it white.

"Why did he draw the cross on his *forehead*?" Dr. Franklin wondered aloud.

"And why paint it white?" Helen asked.

"Do you think these are self-portraits?" the doctor continued. "That Lord Erdely drew himself with a cross on his forehead... because he *had* a cross on his forehead?"

Professor Langer dropped into the chair before the desk and slumped limply. Suddenly he seemed much older.

"He painted what he saw when he looked in the mirror," the professor said.

"Then what's that on his forehead?" Dr. Franklin asked. "Some kind of tattoo?"

"If Lord Erdely had purposely placed a tattoo on his forehead," Charlie argued, "then why did he take such pains to conceal it? In all of his portraits, his forehead is covered by some kind of hat. Why place a tattoo in such a conspicuous place if you want no one to know you have it?"

Professor Langer's words struggled to escape his throat. "It's not a tattoo."

"Then what is it?" Helen asked.

The professor remained unresponsive, as if catatonic, or under some kind of hypnotic spell.

"Professor?" Dr. Franklin finally asked the transfixed Langer.

"Genesis 4:15." The professor's tone was far away. "In the Bible, Cain slew his brother Abel. God placed some kind of mark on Cain. For millennia, scholars have asked, what was that mark?

"In Numbers 12:10, God curses Miriam by striking her with leprosy, turning her 'white as snow'. In Second Kings 5:27, Gehazi and his seed are cursed: also with leprosy. In Second Chronicles 26:19, God curses King Uzziah with leprosy: on his forehead.

"It would seem that when God curses someone, the sign of the curse is snowy white skin.

"The Bible says that God marked Cain to protect him; but many believe that mark was also the sign of his curse. The ancient Babylonians used to place a Tau Cross on the forehead of initiates: just as God marked the cursed Uzziah with leprosy on his forehead. Could this mark on the forehead be the memory of an even more ancient sigla: the mark first placed on the forehead of Cain?"

"A white cross?" Dr. Franklin asked.

"The Mark of Cain."

Charlie struggled to take in what the men were saying. "But how did the mark end up on Lord Erdely's forehead?" he asked.

One of the other guests answered. "We know that Lord Erdely experimented with the black arts. He must have come upon an ancient spell whose significance he did not know. By playing around with the spell, he unwittingly unleashed the curse of Cain on himself."

"That would explain why he kept his forehead covered," Charlie said.

"It would also explain something else," Professor Langer added. "We know that Lord Erdely somehow bound the ears of his servants to keep them from hearing words spoken to them outside the castle: which, unlike words spoken inside the castle, Lord Erdely could not control."

"Why would he not want his servants to hear?"

"It's *what* he did not want them to hear. Erdely was an opponent of Christianity. I think he did not want his servants hearing sacred words. It was his fear of sacred words that made him oppose the Church."

"But why fear sacred words?" Charlie asked.

"The Mark of Cain may have been inert... at first," the professor explained. "It may have required sacred words to 'trigger' it."

"Trigger it?"

"To activate the curse. But, despite Erdely's precautions, it was activated anyway."

"Activated to do what?" asked Dr. Franklin.

Professor Langer paused before responding. "There is a belief among some people that the Mark of Cain has the power to draw to itself the ghosts of murder victims who, like Abel, have gone unavenged."

"'Draw to itself'?"

"Like a magnet, it attracts them."

Dr. Franklin stared at the professor in disbelief. "So you think this servant Charlie has been seeing may be the ghost of someone who died and was called here by Lord Erdely's 'mark'?"

"Not just died—died in the castle."

"Carol Sandu," the doctor muttered.

Professor Langer nodded. "Sandu died in a fire, and Charlie said this servant had a burned face."

"But why is Charlie the only one who can see him?"

The professor chuckled. "Perhaps Charlie is what they call 'sensitive' and has the ability to see spirits."

But Charlie knew there was more to it than that: it was not just that he could *see* this ghost. It had *targeted* him.

Dr. Franklin fixed an open-mouthed stare on Professor Langer. "You're not serious about this, are you?"

Another chuckle. "Do *I* believe it, myself? I am a scholar. Like you, doctor, my method is scientific." An impish gleam twinkled in Langer's eyes. "However, as scientists, isn't it incumbent upon us to keep an open mind?"

"As virtual prisoners in this castle," the doctor said, "it is incumbent upon us to protect ourselves–if... if there really is a madman running loose in the castle."

What had he really been about to say: "If Charlie didn't imagine him"?

Helen, reading Charlie's thoughts, sighed, "Everything's unraveling."

She was right: Charlie could tell from the way Professor Langer and Dr. Franklin looked at him.

"This is a very serious matter, Charlie," the doctor said. "If this is some kind of hoax–or game–of yours, it could have very troubling repercussions. If people start to believe there is a malevolent stranger at large in the castle, it could create panic. And then *real* injuries could ensue."

"I'm not making this up: I *did* see him. He's after me... he's trying to kill me."

"Charlie," Franklin said. "This has to stop."

The pressure inside Charlie's head rose like a crescendo of voices in some mad choir. "I'm telling you," he cried, "something terrible is going to happen!"

Charlie raced from the room, up the cellar stairs, seeking refuge–and maybe safety–in his own room. Locking the door, he prepared to throw himself on the bed.

But he stopped.

Something was *already* on the bed. Cautiously Charlie approached. Inching forth his hand, he picked up the motionless object lying on the blankets.

A gun.

Too weak and dizzy to stand, he sat on the edge of the bed. This gun hadn't been there before. Someone had placed it here while Charlie was out. Who?

An anonymous ally? Some nameless benefactor helping him defend himself? But how would a gun help you defend yourself against a ghost?

Yet what other explanation was there: that the ghost had left the gun? For what conceivable purpose? To further torment him: as it had done with the Tau Cross–the Mark of Cain–painted on Charlie's wall? And with the body hanging from Charlie's ceiling? And with the photograph of Helen in the locket? Why was this malevolent spirit–or whatever it was–doing this? What did it want from Charlie?

Exhausted, Charlie collapsed on the bed, gun in hand, staring blankly at the ceiling. A sea of brown stretched in all directions before his drooping eyes... Pacing an endless brown tunnel, slicing his way through a jungle of whispered echoes... a white figure in the distance: an angel? No, it was Helen, beckoning with her finger.

A crude hand reached out from behind, clutching her shoulder roughly and wrenching her from sight. Charlie had to pursue, had to get her back.

But something was wrong... Charlie could not lift his feet. His shoes were glued to the floor, soles and heels melted by the heat. All around him yellow and orange flames leaped in a macabre witches' dance, circling ever nearer, kicking up a cloud of smoke and soot which engulfed him, invading his nostrils and lungs with suffocating swiftness...

Charlie awoke to a fit of coughing and choking... a reflex from the dream...

Dream...?

What was wrong with his vision? The room was dim, though he couldn't have been sleeping long enough to see evening. Yet his eyes could barely penetrate the smoky...

Smoke.

Charlie leaped to his feet. The fire had already consumed half the room. He had to get out, before his own body was added to the tinder. But a wall of flame barricaded the door.

The window. But even if he could break the thick-paned glass on time (or shoot it out with the gun he still held), the sudden inrush of air would combust the flames with a deadly explosion.

He was trapped.

Strange, the thoughts that pass through your mind when you are about to die. Was the white Tau Cross—the Mark of Cain—glimpsed faintly through the haze on his bedroom wall to be the last image he took with him from this earthly plane? Was he to be a victim of the ancient curse, caught up in the eternal battle between sin and retribution?

Charlie could not restrain a morbid chuckle: Professor Langer had it wrong. He thought the ghost might be the spirit of Carol Sandu. But according to the professor, the Mark of Cain acted like a magnet calling to the ghosts of murder *victims*—and Carol Sandu had not been the victim, but the murderer.

Maybe the professor had it backwards: maybe the Mark of Cain was not a magnet to unavenged murder victims, but to the *murderers* whose crimes had gone unavenged...

No, that wouldn't make any sense...

60

A confused muddle of thoughts crowded Charlie's brain, as if the flood of smoke outside his head were seeping inside. The professor's words ricocheted aimlessly off the walls of Charlie's mind: Carol Sandu strangling Ileana Anca in jealous protest of her feelings for Emilian... Lord Erdely's Mark of Cain summoning the restless spirits of the dead... A relentless torment at the hands of a non-existent servant with a burned face... Burned in the fire that had consumed this very room thirty years ago? (Remember the charred walls you found behind the wallpaper this morning?)... The pain and panic of not being able to take another breath...

Reflexively Charlie raced, navigating as best he could, to the far side of the bed. Holstering the gun in his back pocket, he tossed himself against the wall beyond the bed's foot. His hands groped rapidly among the boards, pressing blindly on the wooden panels. It was there, he knew it was... it had to be: the one key wall panel that would yield. He could not tell if it was the fever of anxiety or the rapid encroachment of flames that was burning his body both within and without.

He heard the click at the same time as the wooden slat retreated from his fingers. He knew without seeing that as the panel had receded into the wall, a hidden door had somewhere been released.

Wildly Charlie felt for an uneven surface—and when his hands struck the protruding edge of the secret doorway, his fingers dug desperately into the seam. Lungs filled with smoke left him too weak to drag the edge of the heavy wooden door even the inches he would need to squeeze through the opening. Then a surge of hysteria amplified what small energy remained in him, to a level barely exceeding the resistance of the door. With a squeal nearly drowned by the hissing flames, the revolving partition protested its enforced compliance, striking Charlie's sweat-drenched face with a blast of chilly air from an unseen, newly-formed opening.

Madly, Charlie pressed against the cleft in the wall, forcing his body through a space half its girth.

Shimmering haze was suddenly replaced by icy blackness. Charlie stood shivering in an unlit passageway behind the wall. But fear of the known outweighed that of the unknown, and Charlie's only thought was to distance himself from the inferno he had so narrowly escaped. His footsteps echoed eerily as he wound his way through the dark corridor, until choked off abruptly by the obstruction of a dead end.

It's *not* a dead end, Charlie told himself. Like a frantic mime's, his flattened palms traced a rectangular patch of rough wooden wall, seeking its Achilles heel. At length he felt a section of wall recoil, and the cool, stale air lent him strength to wedge it open.

He pressed through to find himself in the hidden study Dr. Franklin had found this morning outside Charlie's room at the end of the corridor. The secret door in the wall–released by the hook behind the portrait–still stood ajar. Before he even had time to glance around the room, Charlie's breath caught in his throat.

He was not alone.

Across the room, the man in servant's livery, with the burnt face, stared directly at him.

The specter grinned malevolently. "They call you Charlie," it said in a deep, sandpaper voice.

"You can talk!" Charlie exclaimed.

"Of course."

"In English."

"They taught it in the schools. Plus, I have had years to improve: so many American tourists are drawn to Transylvania, for some reason."

Charlie's perspiring lip quivered. "What is it you want with me?"

"I want you to suffer."

Charlie's head began to spin. "Suffer? Why? I don't even know you."

"Don't you?"

As menacing as the words were, Charlie was more unsettled by the intensity with which the ghost–or whatever it was–stared at him. A stare that seemed somehow familiar...

"Charlie?"

A voice from behind. Helen's. Helen stood inside the study, beside the hallway door.

"Charlie, what happened? Your room is on fire. The others are putting it out."

Through the door Charlie heard the sound of fire extinguishers and frantic voices screaming instructions.

"*You* did this," Charlie said to the ghost. "You set that fire. You did all of it: you put this gun in my room." Charlie removed the gun from his back pocket and brandished it before the spirit. "You painted that white cross–the Mark of Cain–on my bedroom wall." The charfaced figure acknowledged the charges with a silent nod. "But why?"

"Because," the specter said, "there are some things in this world– and beyond it–that you can never escape."

Helen looked on fearfully, speaking with overwhelmed emotion. "What's going on, Charlie?"

From the corridor outside Charlie heard voices announce that the fire seemed to be under control.

"We could use some help over here," a muffled voice called from Charlie's room.

"Wait... I thought I heard something."

"Heard something?"

"Voices... from that hidden study you found this morning, Doc."

"You think there's someone in there?"

"I'll go check."

"Wait, Langer, it could be our arsonist. I'll go with you."

Charlie waited to see what the ghost would do. Would it flee from the sound of the men making their way into the room; or would it scoff, having nothing to fear from those who would not know it was there?

"Charlie, what happened?" exclaimed Dr. Franklin as he and Professor Langer swept past Helen through the hallway door. The doctor stared at Charlie's browned and sooty clothing.

But Professor Langer was looking *past* Charlie, in the direction of the liveried apparition. He pointed at the man Charlie was certain only he himself could see.

"Who's *that?*" the professor asked.

"You can see him?" Charlie cried.

"Of course I can see him."

Charlie expected a wave of exhilaration to sweep over him: at last he was vindicated. He was not crazy, after all. Yet Charlie suddenly realized that when the ghost ceased to be Charlie's own private "possession", as it were, a certain indefinable safety and control slipped from his grasp. Charlie was now at the mercy of whatever events ensued.

Dr. Franklin seemed to be able to see the ghost, as well; for he looked directly at it and called out, "Who are you? What are you doing here?"

In its deep, resonating voice, the ghost replied, "My name is Emilian."

A moment of frowning reflection, and then the doctor's face beamed with recognition. "Emilian... you were one of the patients of the asylum thirty years ago." Slowly Dr. Franklin put together the pieces. "Carol Sandu's rival for the affection of Ileana Anca. It was out of jealousy of Ileana's feelings for you that Sandu strangled her with a curtain sash and then set fire to her room."

"When I saw the flames, I burst into her room to try and save her." Emilian himself seemed haunted by the ghost of her memory. "I didn't know he had already killed her."

63

"That's how your face got burned," Dr. Franklin realized.

"Poor man," Helen whispered.

"So *you* must be our castle 'ghost'," Professor Langer said.

"You lived here thirty years ago," added the doctor, "so you are familiar with the castle's secret passages–like the one we found in Charlie's room just now. That's how you were able to disappear into thin air, and enter and leave Charlie's room, with the door and window locked."

"But why?" Professor Langer asked. "Why have you been persecuting Charlie?"

Helen was staring slack-jawed at Emilian. "After the asylum closed, you stayed on as a servant," she said. "But why?"

"He couldn't shake the memory of his lost love," Charlie answered for Emilian.

"That may well be true," replied Dr. Franklin in a tone inexplicably impatient and patronizing. "But it doesn't answer the question: why harass *you*, Charlie?"

"Are you sure you're all right, Charlie?" Professor Langer asked in a concerned tone.

Emilian fixed cold, relentless eyes on Charlie. "It was fate that brought you here," he said.

"*I* brought him here," Helen insisted. "This was all my fault."

"Don't blame yourself," Charlie told her. "I wanted to come."

Like reflections in a mirror, Dr. Franklin and Professor Langer echoed the same stupefied expression.

"Who are you talking to?" the doctor asked Charlie.

Charlie pointed to Helen. "Her."

"*Who?*"

"Helen. Helen Grace. Standing next to the door."

"There's no one next to the door, Charlie," Professor Langer said. "We–you, me, the doctor, and Emilian–are the only ones in this room."

Everything began to spin.

"But... but..."

Why couldn't they see her?

"Wait a minute," the professor said suddenly. "Did you say 'Helen Grace'?" Charlie could not find his tongue; and only the most desperate effort could force his head to nod. "Of course! Why didn't I realize it before?"

"Realize what?" asked the doctor.

"The names. My Romanian may be weak, but it was good enough to translate the names."

"Names? What names?"

"The names of the patients. The patients of the asylum thirty years ago."

"You mean, like Carol Sandu?"

"'Carol' is Romanian for Charles. 'Sandu' is a shortened form of Alexandru: or Alexander. Carol Sandu, translated into English, becomes—"

"Charlie Alexander."

"I didn't realize it until just now, when Charlie mentioned someone named 'Helen Grace'."

"Who's Helen Grace?"

"The female patient whom Carol Sandu strangled with a curtain sash thirty years ago was named Ileana Anca. 'Ileana' is the Romanian form of 'Helen'; 'Anca' is Romanian for 'Grace'. 'Helen Grace' is the young woman killed here thirty years ago."

"So this 'Helen Grace' Charlie mentioned is—"

"The hallucination of a woman who's been dead for thirty years."

Charlie wasn't listening. He couldn't bear to listen. Yet a part of him could not help but hear. After all, Helen was twenty-five years old: thirty years younger than Charlie. The age Ileana had been when she was killed thirty years ago. The locket Emilian left for them–for him–contained a photograph of Ileana taken thirty years ago: which was why the locket looked so old. Yet the picture was identical to the current appearance of Helen Grace... who was twenty-five when Charlie first met her... thirty years ago...

Dr. Franklin seemed to be groping through fogs of understanding. "So Charlie is really—"

"Carol Sandu."

So *that* was what Emilian–Charlie's erstwhile "ghost"–had cried out at the top of the staircase. What had sounded like "Colonel Sanders" was Charlie's name: his real, Romanian name. Carol Sandu.

Dr. Franklin nodded slowly. "That would explain certain things."

Professor Langer cocked his head. "Such as?"

"When we first arrived here at the castle, we encountered a step at the threshold of the front door which is impossible to see. The only reason we didn't all trip on it is because Mrs. Harris, the *second* person to pass through, tripped over it herself, alerting us to its existence. But Charlie, the first to enter the castle, *didn't* trip over it. Why not? *Because he already knew it was there*, having lived in the castle thirty years ago."

65

Professor Langer nodded slowly. "It makes sense. When we were searching this room this morning, it was *Charlie* who found the secret alcove that contained the drawings. Undoubtedly because he is familiar with all the castle's secret nooks and crannies."

Through the haze of confusion Emilian's voice reached toward Charlie. "When they closed the asylum, the patients were relocated. Some, like me, were reintegrated into society. I was allowed to stay on as a servant.

"The servants are supposed to complete their duties and leave the castle before the guests arrive. But I fell behind. Imagine my surprise when I found myself face to face with Carol Sandu, supposedly burned to death in a fire thirty years ago. The man who murdered the woman I loved."

Images long ago erased by blinding pain, like film exposed to blazing sunlight, began to rematerialize in Charlie's mind. Ileana's frail quivering body drained of life as he tightened the horrid green curtain sash around her neck. Trauma had done something to his mind, devouring that part of his life like a tidal wave swallows a weary swimmer. The doctors here had called forgotten memories like that—what was the English word? *Repression?*

"When I saw you," Emilian continued, "I realized what must have happened. After you murdered Ileana, you set her room on fire: partly to cover up the true cause of her death, but mostly to simulate your own. You escaped from her room through the secret passage. Everyone assumed you were consumed in the fire, so no one went looking for you. While you apparently fled to America."

"But when you saw me this morning—"

"I realized the truth."

"So you led me to Ileana's room on purpose this morning."

"I couldn't let you go unpunished. I couldn't let you forget."

"That was the purpose of the hanging effigy you strung up in my room."

"Strangled by a cord. Like poor Ileana."

"You put the curtains back up after I took them down."

"You cannot hide your guilt. Even from yourself. I won't let you."

"And the Mark of Cain painted on my wall—"

"I tried to make everything look like the work of a ghost. I wanted you to be as haunted as I have been."

"So it *was* you who set my room on fire."

"You should have died in that fire. Why should my Ileana die, and her murderer live?"

66

He was right, of course. In his rage thirty years ago, Charlie had seen *himself* as victim. But like a dazzling flash of lightning at midnight, Emilian's words opened Charlie's eyes. The enormity of Charlie's deed overwhelmed him, the avalanche of unalterable fact burying the irretrievably lost memory of innocence.

"I'm leaving now." Helen started to fade. "And there is only one way to follow me. You know what you have to do."

For thirty years Charlie had been running from this moment... only to end up here. And he was too tired to run any longer.

He put the gun to his temple.

"No!" cried Dr. Franklin.

But it was too late. The explosion, and Helen's indistinct words, were the last sounds Charlie heard in this world.

Dr. Franklin raced to the motionless body on the floor. Kneeling in a pool of blood, he frantically searched Charlie's neck for a pulse.

The doctor shook his head in vexed resignation. "He's gone."

Professor Langer looked coldly at Emilian. "That's why you gave him the gun."

Emilian spoke without emotion. "He owed God a life."

"Hadn't he paid already?" the doctor demanded. "For thirty years he was wracked with guilt. So much that he hallucinated the girl he had murdered."

Emilian shook his head. "That's denial, not guilt."

"Unless," suggested Professor Langer, "it was no hallucination."

"What are you talking about?" snapped Dr. Franklin.

"Well, to give the Devil his due, Erdely Castle has fallen under the influence of the Mark of Cain: a mark, legend tells us, that attracts the spirits of unavenged murder victims. How do we know Ileana Anca wasn't one such spirit, drawn here by the Mark... towing Charlie Alexander in her wake?"

"To answer for his crime," Emilian added.

"Don't be ridiculous," Dr. Franklin protested. "Helen Grace was a hallucination, not a ghost. A projection of Charlie's guilt, nothing more."

Professor Langer chuckled. "What happened to the open-minded man of science, doctor?"

"He was mentored by the realist," Franklin said.

The professor's amused laughter gave place to sober pragmatism. "Well, I suppose someone should go inform Miss Brooks what happened here."

With little relish for the task, Professor Langer headed toward the hallway door.

"Hey, what the..." he cried, struggling to regain his balance as he nearly fell headlong to the floor.

"What is it?" Dr. Franklin called out anxiously.

"I stepped on something... nearly tripped..."

Professor Langer stooped to pick an object off the floor, holding it before his face with curious expression.

"What is it?" asked the doctor.

Professor Langer held the item out before him. Tied in a bow.

A pink hair ribbon.

AUTHOR'S BIO:

Eric Keith is a designer of logical puzzles. This is his first published work. Hopefully not his last.

"I dedicate this story to my wife Marcia, because she dedicated her last story to me; and more importantly, for her toleration, and for introducing me to Lea Schizas."

A Mother's Love
By
Marcia Berneger

"I'm not going!"

"You're going, young lady! I'm not leaving a child home alone for an entire week!"

"I'm not a child. I'm sixteen, and there's no way I'm going to some God-forsaken town in Romania, or anywhere else with you! I've got plans for this week, and I'll be damned if I'm canceling them for you."

"Watch your language, young lady."

Samantha ignored her mother's warning. There was never anything behind her threats, anyway. "What's the big deal about this stupid town anyway? Why do you have to go now?"

"We own some land right outside the town. Apparently they've found some highly toxic residue in the pond on our land and they're going to charge us some enormous fee if I don't get the mess cleaned up immediately."

"How'd we wind up with land in... in... ?"

"Cornifu. It was passed down to us from relatives dating way back."

"Back to Great-great Grandma... what's her name? The one you won't let anyone talk about? What's up with that, anyway?"

"Never you mind! Just start packing. We leave in the morning!"

"We leave in the morning," mimicked Samantha, throwing herself onto her bed. "This whole thing sucks!" she shouted, fighting back tears. "Just wait 'till I'm eighteen. I'll be out of your hair forever!"

Samantha hated her mother. She hated being treated like a child. Samantha was supposed to stay back in Los Angeles with her Aunt Jenny while her mother went to Romania. Aunt Jenny was cool—no curfew, no shouting at her day and night. But the plans fell through when Aunt Jenny changed her mind and decided to go on a stupid cruise during the exact same week!

"You'll get to go to Europe!" Aunt Jenny said, smiling. "What a lucky girl!"

"You don't get it! I can't stand living in the same house with my mother. How do you expect me to stay in a tiny hotel room with her?" Samantha sobbed, twirling her beaded bracelet in agitation. No one understood!

* * * *

They arrived in Romania the following Friday and checked into the tiny hotel.   As soon as her mother left to meet with the property lawyer, Samantha grabbed her cell phone to call her boyfriend.

"Oh, my God. No service available! What kind of hell hole did she stick us in?" Samantha flung herself on the bed. Reaching over, she picked up the hotel phone. "I'd like to place a call to California, please."

After an hour of trying to get someone to understand her, the phone finally rang through to Los Angeles.

"Robert? Robert, it's so good to talk to you. I... what's going on? Who's there with you? Robert, there's a girl there. What? You can't... Fine! Don't *ever* talk to me again!" Samantha slammed the phone down. "No one cares about me at all!" she shouted. "Nothing ever goes right in my life!"

* * * *

But then the invitation arrived. Samantha had discovered it after her shower. Someone had slipped it under their door. Although addressed to Mrs. Sarina Jamison, boredom, tinged with anger, prodded Samantha to open the envelope and read its contents.

Eyes wide with excitement and anticipation, Samantha read and re-read the invitation. A haunted castle! A real haunted castle! How perfect, especially here in Transylvania. Spooky town, Dracula town. She couldn't wait to tell her mother. They'd been invited to visit an honest-to-goodness haunted castle!

"You're not going," her mother said.

"What do you mean, I'm not going? This is the first really cool thing to have happened. Mom, it's a real castle!"

"I'm not even sure I'm going. But even if I do, you are definitely not coming with me. Not to that castle."

"Why? What's wrong with this castle? You're not afraid it's haunted, are you? You don't believe in that stuff. You're always telling me so." Samantha pursed her lips. "Does this have something to do with my great-great grandmother? Wait a minute--wasn't there some scandal about her and some Lord back then... Lord Eddie or something?"

But her mother was adamant. No discussion. Samantha could not go.

She had not expected her mother to say no. She'd have to find another way to get there.

71

The invitation said a bus would pick everyone up at 8:00 A.M. Sheesh! Samantha was definitely not a morning person. But she was determined to go.

Mom's alarm woke them both at 6:30. Samantha rolled over and pretended to go back to sleep while her mom showered and dressed. As soon as Mom left for breakfast, Samantha bolted out of bed, threw on some black jeans and a long-sleeved shirt, grabbed her black-fringed shawl and headed out the door, pausing only long enough to slip on her boots and leave a quick note saying she went out to explore the town. She raced down the back stairs. Checking the dining room to be sure her mom hadn't finished eating, Samantha slunk through the lobby and left the hotel. It was a quarter to eight.

Glancing around, Samantha finally located the tour bus parked behind the hotel. Shrouding her head and face with her shawl, the teen casually strolled toward the bus. Her heart thumped wildly as the driver walked toward her, a clipboard and pen in his hands.

But the driver passed by without even glancing as he walked toward the hotel to pick up the guests. Samantha didn't have much time.

Samantha made her way toward the back of the bus, glad the door was left open wide enough for her to slip through. She chose a seat by a broken window and ducked down into it. Once the bus was on its way, Samantha would be safe. She began to relax.

The old castle was even more spectacular than Samantha had imagined. She remained on the bus until everyone had gotten off, panicking when the driver closed the door as he left to lead the guests toward the castle.

The teen tried prying the doors open, then pounded on them when they failed to budge. What if she were trapped there all day? She watched as the last guest entered the castle. Suddenly the bus door opened—all by itself. Samantha stepped outside the bus, gaping at the magnificent view before her. Even in daylight, it was awesome: huge towering walls, powerfully built crenellations and turrets... everything Samantha had ever read about was right in front of her.

A chilling wind whipped at her shawl. Samantha peered skyward. The sun-drenched morning had given way to a gray dreariness. The smell of rain now filled the air. Samantha hurried toward the massive wooden front doors. Pulling with all her strength, she could not budge the doors. She circled to the right, hoping to find an open window, but to no avail. Tears of frustration threatened to overtake her as she rounded side after side of endless castle walls. A second, smaller door appeared. Samantha reached for its ornate bronze handle. She jumped back as the door opened, just wide enough for her to pass through.

It slammed shut behind her.

"And in here we have the kitchen..." The tour guide turned and let out a scream as she saw a black figure near the back door.

"Oh, man!" moaned Samantha. "Busted!" She turned to grab the back door and escape.

"That won't help you, Missy," said the guide, recovering from her shock. "That door has been frozen shut for decades."

The teen turned to dispute this information.

"Samantha!" an angry voice blared out. Mrs. Jamison moved toward her daughter, yanking the shawl from her face.

Samantha's shoulders sagged. "I thought you weren't going to come?"

"Just what do you think you're doing here? How did you get here, anyway?" She turned to face the tour guide. "Miss Brooks, I'm so sorry..."

Suddenly, a loud crash shook the castle. Several screams rang out in response.

"Relax, ladies and gentlemen. We're just experiencing a bit of a storm." Miss Brooks's voice belied her confidence. "It should pass harmlessly by in an hour or so. Let's continue the tour."

"I'll deal with you later!" Mrs. Jamison whispered through gritted teeth. She grabbed her daughter's wrist. "You stay right by my side. You hear me?"

"Yes, Mother," Samantha mumbled. She stared down at the wooden floorboards as they walked. She was soon dragging her feet, bored by the tour. She fiddled with the beads on her bracelet.

"...probably a 17th century portrait of... furniture dating back to the 16th century..." On and on Miss Brooks droned, her words punctuated by an occasional thunderclap.

Samantha longed to wander about the castle on her own.

The group ascended the marble staircase, pausing in the middle to stare at a large portrait of a young man. He wore festive clothing dating back to the Renaissance. Samantha recognized the style.

"...Lord Erdely..."

Samantha's ears perked up. "Lord Erdely, that was the name!" she whispered.

"... lived in the early 1600's... pretty strict with his many servants... disappeared in 1654... assumed to have died."

"Why is he so sad?" interrupted Samantha.

"All of the portraits of Lord Erdely were painted that way. He always appears with that same forlorn, lonely countenance," explained Miss Brooks.

"Maybe he lost his one true love?" Samantha said, thoughtfully.

"Some people believe his ghost haunts the castle."

"Perhaps he's looking for her." Samantha smiled up at the portrait.

"Just in case, watch where you sit. You don't want to find yourself on Lord Erdely's lap."

Samantha frowned in disgust as the group of unbelievers snickered. *Go ahead and laugh!* the teen thought. *Just give me a day or two here! I'd show them. I'd find the ghost and prove them all wrong!*

The lights flickered. An icy breeze floated through the room, followed by the entrance of a short man in mud-splattered work clothes. Looking at the group of tourists with concerned eyes and wrinkled brow, he whispered something to Miss Brooks. A short, heated argument ensued. No one understood the Romanian banter, only that something unexpected and disturbing had occurred.

The guide's face clouded with worry. She turned to face her guests as the workman departed, slamming the massive front door behind him. The icy chill remained in the room.

"Ladies and gentlemen," the guide began. "Apparently this storm is worse than I had thought. All roads leading to Lord Erdely's castle are washed out."

A low murmur arose from the guests. The guide held up her hands for silence.

"It seems..." she cleared her throat nervously, "...it seems we will need to remain here for a few days until work trucks can be brought in to clear the roads. But don't worry. There are enough rooms for everyone and the kitchen is well-stocked. You will be quite comfortable during your short stay. And there will be no charge, of course."

The whispering of the guests turned to a loud grumbling. Several took out cell phones, only to discover, as Samantha already knew from her hotel imprisonment, there was no reception in this remote village. They were all isolated in the huge castle, stuck for the next two days.

"Yes!" whispered Samantha. Just what she'd wished for. The lights flickered again, as if in agreement.

The guests were escorted to their rooms.

"But why do we have to share a room?" whined Samantha when she and her mother were assigned one of the chambers. "There's more than enough places for me to bunk by myself!"

"Because I'm going to keep my eye on you. You can't just go wandering around this mansion by yourself! You'll get lost."

"It's a castle, Mom, not a mansion. And we're stuck here for two nights. I'm not spending them locked in this room with you!"

Mrs. Jamison glared at her daughter, hands firmly planted on her hips. "You'll do what I tell you."

Samantha tried a different approach. "Anyway, there's a ton of history tied up here. You heard the guide. The artwork, the furniture, even Lord Erdely himself. Miss Brooks certainly described enough for me to write about... and get extra credit for my world history class." Samantha looked up hopefully. "It would help bring my grade up." The teen raised her eyebrows and flashed her mom a smile.

"It's against my better judgment," Mom sighed, "but as long as you show up at every meal..."

"Mom, you are so cool!"

"And are back in the room by 8:00 at night."

"Ten o'clock."

"Nine!"

"Deal!" Samantha grinned. That had been easier than she expected. She bolted from the room and raced down the hall.

Samantha wandered from room to room. "This is so much better than any dumb history class!" she shouted to the pictures on the wall of a large, ornately furnished bedroom. The huge, oak four-corner bed took up almost the entire room. The teen walked over to a large portrait on the side wall. She glanced up at the life-size image of an older gentleman, dressed in royal blue waistcoat and pants, white ruffled shirt and tall plumed hat.

"I wonder if that's Lord Erdely?" Samantha whispered, staring up at his hauntingly lonely eyes. A shadow suddenly crossed over the figure. Samantha turned, but she was still alone in the room. She returned her gaze to the portrait, captivated by a calmness radiating from the man's face, something she had missed before. The shadow was gone.

Whoa! That was weird. Samantha hurried from the room, drawing her shawl tightly around her. Thinking it must be close to dinnertime, the teen headed toward the salon. She glanced behind periodically, unable to shake the feeling she was being followed.

"Samantha!" A hand grabbed her shoulder.

The girl jumped and whirled around, right into her mother.

"Geez, Mom! You nearly gave me a heart attack!"

"Don't tell me this house has you spooked?" Mom laughed.

"It's not funny! Something's not right here. I can feel it. Just ask that bizarre man from the tour, Mr. Alexander. Even *he* thinks something weird is going on."

"If you ask me, he's the weird one. I passed by his room on the way over. He was having a whole conversation with himself."

"Maybe he was talking to a ghost?" Samantha grinned at her mother. "Just because you don't believe..."

"Just the same, I think you should stay close to me tonight." Mom reached to put her arm around her daughter.

"No, thanks. I'm fine." Samantha ducked out of the approaching embrace. "I just came to see if it was dinnertime. I didn't want to be late."

"I was just heading there myself." Mom sighed. "We can walk together."

They entered the enormous dining room. Her mother went to check out the food situation in the kitchen. Samantha took a seat in an empty, high back mahogany chair. She stood to scoot it closer to the table. The chair pushed gently forward, bumping her legs and plopping her into the seat.

"Thanks," Samantha said, turning.

"Who are you thanking?" asked Mom as she approached, carrying a plate of turkey sandwiches in one hand and a pitcher of ice tea in the other.

"Um... you, of course, for bringing dinner in." Samantha glanced around as the guests filed in for dinner, some clearly upset at having to fix their own meal.

"Being stuck in this cold, drafty castle is bad enough," grumbled a large man, rubbing the top of his balding head. "Someone should be serving us, taking care of us!"

"I agree, dear. I can't wait to leave. This place gives me the creeps!"

"You're not believing all this nonsense about the castle being haunted, are you?"

"No, of course not." She glanced back toward the salon. "But did you notice the portraits back there?"

"Of Lord Erdely? Poor lonely, wretched soul. What about them?"

"Take a look after dinner. He doesn't appear to be quite as lonely now."

"What? Deary, you're letting your imagination run wild."

"Maybe he's happy because we're all here to keep him company!" chuckled Professor Langer. Everyone laughed and the tension around the room eased.

Samantha could barely choke down half a sandwich.

"May I be excused, Mom?" she said, shoving her chair back so quickly it nearly toppled over.

"Yes, dear, but remember to be back by 9:00."

Samantha headed for the salon and scrutinized the portraits. The fat, bald man was right. The three portraits, all of Lord Erdely at different ages, had indeed changed. The youngest figure, a teen about Samantha's age, stared now with eyes filled with hope. The next, portraying Lord Erdely in his twenties, a deep yearning etched in his face, and the last, an older version similar to the one in the bedroom, seemed to have... Samantha stared, blinked, and checked again. Yes, there absolutely was a twinkle in those eyes.

Lord Erdely was definitely there in the castle, or at least his spirit was. She would find him, get to know him, and convince him to show himself to her mother. *Mr. Alexander won't be the only one seeing a ghost!* she thought, smugly.

Samantha looked down at her black outfit. "I can't meet a Lord in this!" she muttered, frowning. She returned to her room to check the closets, hoping to find something more suitable, more periodic, left there, maybe, for tourists to see.

She flung open the massive wardrobe doors, only to be disappointed by the emptiness inside.

Turning to leave, she caught sight of it lying across her bed: an authentic, absolutely exquisite Renaissance dress, complete with shoes, long white gloves and ivory cameo pendant on a silver chain. Samantha changed quickly, then made her way back to the bedroom containing Lord Erdely's portrait.

Samantha curtsied, bowing her head. "Thank you, Lord Erdely."

"You're welcome, dear Samantha," boomed a deep voice from behind.

A chill shivered down her spine as the teen slowly turned. Standing before her was a tall, stately figure. "Lord Erdely," whispered Samantha.

The figure bowed graciously before her, then took her hand and gently kissed it. Their eyes met. Samantha gasped. There was such longing in those deep blue eyes, such passion. The girl pulled her hand away and stepped back, her cheeks burning.

"I did not mean to embarrass you, my dear. It's just..." Lord Erdely sighed before continuing. "You are such a beautiful woman."

Samantha was unsure what to do. This was what she had wanted— to meet the ghost, to prove to her mother that he was real. But, Lord Erdely was so kind, so... so magnificent. She didn't want to share him with anyone.

Lord Erdely interrupted her thoughts. "Would you allow me the honor of showing you around my home?"

"That would be great!" she said, linking her arm around his. They strolled through the upper halls undisturbed.

Everyone must still be at dinner, Samantha thought as they stopped to enter a small bedroom. She gazed around the beautiful little room. A delicate pink canopy shaded the small white-laced bed. She walked over to the plain pine hope chest resting in the corner. A washbasin and pitcher caught her eye. She dipped her fingers in the water puddled in the bottom of the basin.

"It's warm," she said, surprised.

"I keep it ready."

Samantha withdrew her hand, shaking off the wetness. "Ready for what?"

Lord Erdely offered no response.

"Whose room was this?"

"It belonged to the head housekeeper and her young daughter." He held out his hand. "Come, there are many more rooms to see."

Samantha moved to the short bureau on the wall opposite the door. She glanced at the two small portraits resting on the lace runner. One was of a tall, vaguely familiar-looking woman dressed in a servant's uniform, her arm around a young girl. The second portrait was of Lord Erdely.

Samantha frowned, wondering why his picture would be in the servant's room. She picked up the other portrait and stared at the two figures. The girl appeared to be around her own age, with long black hair fixed in ringlets. The face was too tiny for Samantha to make out any details, only that the daughter resembled the mother.

It was the mother that intrigued Samantha. She had seen that face, those soft green eyes... if she could only remember where.

"Her name was Sarah," Lord Erdely explained, looking over Samantha's shoulder. "She was a courageous woman. When her daughter was accused by the villagers of being a witch, her mother came forward and confessed. The daughter's life was spared. But Sarah..." Lord Erdely removed the portrait from the teen's hand and placed it back on the bureau. "We need to go, Samantha," he said. "It is almost 9:00."

"But I don't want to stop. We haven't seen the whole castle yet." Samantha turned to face the ghostly figure. "I have a million questions to ask. What's it like being dead? What's it like being a ghost? Can you walk through walls? How come I can see you? Can other people..."

"Steady there, young lady. I'll come again tomorrow. I'll answer your questions then. We have much to discuss." Lord Erdely smiled. "I will answer one question now. You can see me because you want to. But if we don't get you back on time, your mother will not be likely to set you free tomorrow."

"Okay, I get it. Let's go."

They passed by a bedroom with a large portrait. Lord Erdely stopped. "I must stay here." He entered the room and moved toward the far wall. He gazed up and smiled. "This was the last portrait of me before... before I left. It is my favorite."

Samantha looked up. The portrait was of Lord Erdely as he now appeared, a distinguished older gentleman, neatly trimmed white whiskers and long handlebar mustache, smart-looking blue and white uniform. Samantha could really fall for him, if he were a lot younger.

"Samantha?"

"Rats!" The teen walked toward the doorway. "Coming, Mother," she called. She turned to say goodnight, but Lord Erdely had vanished. She glanced up at the portrait.

"What the...?" Samantha blinked and stared at the picture again. There was a shadow in the portrait, a fuzzy figure standing next to Lord Erdely. Was that there before?

"Now, Samantha! It's 9:15."

"All right. I'm coming!" The girl ran to the bedroom door, breezed by her mother and locked herself in the bathroom. Her head spun from her evening's adventure. Eventually, she removed the dress and crawled into her bed. She'd get to the bottom of everything in the morning.

Samantha's dreams were filled with fairy-tale princes carrying her off to far-away castles. Tall princes in blue and white uniforms...

Samantha awoke more confused than ever.

"Where did that fancy dress come from?" Mom asked at breakfast.

"I found it in the bedroom closet. I hung it back up last night."

"The necklace, too?"

Samantha's hand flew to her neck. She'd forgotten about the cameo. "It was with the dress. I'll put it back before we leave."

"I don't think you should continue wearing it. What if you lose it?"

Samantha scowled and pushed back her chair. "Did they say if we could leave today?"

As if in response, thunder boomed overhead and the lights flickered.

"Not that I want to, of course!" Samantha added, glancing around.

"What did you do last night all by yourself?" asked Mom, placing her hand on her daughter's shoulder to get her attention.

Samantha shuddered. She was still trying to figure it all out. Maybe she dreamed it all? No, she thought as she fingered the necklace. Last night was real.

Samantha looked around the table. Maybe someone was messing

with her. Her eyes narrowed as she pouted. Stupid! Of course, that was it. Maybe it was that weirdo, Mr. Alexander. First he pretends to see a ghost, just to scare everyone and set her up. Then he dresses as Lord Erdely, masquerading as his ghost. He really had her going. If he tried that again today, she'd be ready.

"Samantha!" Mom sounded worried.

The teen snapped out of her daze. "What?" She looked up. "Oh, last night? Nothing. I didn't do anything. Just roamed around. You know, took a tour of the castle, danced with Lord Erdely. Nothing out of the ordinary."

"Well, just behave yourself. Don't touch anything we can't afford to replace."

Samantha shook herself free from her mother's grasp and strode angrily from the room. "She never really listens to me," she muttered. "I could've said I'd killed someone and she'd have said, 'That's nice, dear' or something just as dumb."

Samantha rounded a corner and stopped. *He* was there, at the end of the corridor, staring at her.

"How dare you!" shouted Samantha as she stormed toward the figure. He stood his ground as the girl approached.

"I know who you really are... Mr. Alexander. You don't fool me!"

A door opened. Samantha jumped as an old man popped his head out. "Who are you yelling at?" squawked the old grouch.

"Mr. Alexander." The teen pointed down the hallway.

The old man glanced at the empty corridor. "Not you, too." He peered at the girl. "I don't know what's gotten into everyone here. First Alexander sees a ghost, now you. Well, you be careful, young lady." He shook his crooked finger in her face. "Alexander is dead. Don't you be the next victim." He pulled his head back and slammed his door.

Samantha stared at the door. "He's dead? Mr. Alexander is dead?" She turned back down the hallway. "Then who..." she asked the figure beckoning to her, "are you?"

As if in a dream, Samantha half-walked, half-floated toward the stately figure.

"I would never deceive you, fair Samantha. I am Lord Erdely. I have been on such a long quest. At last I have found what I have sought for centuries."

"What were you seeking?" Samantha's voice quivered.

"My one true love. I lost her the day I... disappeared. I knew she would return to me one day." He gazed longingly into her eyes. "And now, she has."

Lord Erdely took her hands gently into his own. "You feel it too, don't you... a connection to the past? My past? I knew you sensed it when you picked up that portrait on the bureau."

Samantha looked up, confused. "Portrait?"

"Sarah's portrait. Why, you're even named after her. I knew if I waited long enough, she would come back to me. And she has, through you, her granddaughter."

"But Sarah must have lived centuries ago. I can't be her granddaughter."

"Time means nothing to me here. Though generations apart, you are still her descendent and therefore bear a resemblance to her physical beauty as well as her spirit. Stay with me, fair Samantha. I will love you and care for you. I..."

"Samantha!"

Her mother's voice broke the spell. Samantha shook her head, trying to clear her thoughts.

"There you are. I've been searching all over for you."

Samantha focused on the figure marching down the hall. Her mother was angry. What had she done now?

"You missed lunch, young lady. You've broken our deal!"

"Lunch?" Samantha frowned. "What are you talking about? It's only..." She glanced around for a clock.

"It's almost 2:00. Lunch was over almost an hour ago. That's it! You're grounded. You're to stay in your room until dinner."

"But Mom, you don't understand. I've been with..."

"I don't care who you've found to hang around with. No one here wants to be bothered by a pesky child, anyway. Now hustle back to the room."

"Is that all I am to you? A pesky child? First Aunt Jenny abandons me, then Robert dumps me, and now the real shocker--you don't give a damn about me either. Nobody cares about me. I could die tomorrow and I'd just be an inconvenience to walk around."

"Stop feeling sorry for yourself. Now get going!"

Samantha shoved past her mother, fuming.

"And take off that necklace when you get to the room!"

"I'll show you. I'll show you all!" Samantha strode purposefully down the hall, brushing hot tears from her cheeks. Slamming the door as she entered the room, the teen opened the wardrobe. Trembling, she replaced her clothes with the lace dress, pulling it slowly over her head. "There's nothing for me in this world," she sobbed as she fastened the dress hooks.

81

The bedroom door opened. Sarina Jamison entered, pale and shaky. "Honey," she whispered.

"What's the matter, Mother? You look like you've seen a ghost," sneered her daughter.

"I'm not sure what I just saw. I was passing the large blue bedroom down the hall when something drew me inside. There's a picture of Lord Erdely..."

"I know. I've seen it."

"In the picture there's a girl next to him. It's too blurred to make out, but the girl appears to be wearing..." her mother suddenly focused on her daughter. "Wearing the dress you have on. I thought I told you not to wear that. Take it off!" Her voice grew loud and shrill. "Take it off now!"

"No, I won't take it off. I won't do anything you say anymore. I don't even want to be around you. You don't understand what's going on and you don't want to. Nobody cares what I want—not you, not Robert, not Aunt Jenny. Well, I know someone who does care. He's asked me to stay with him. And I'm going to find him and tell him yes!"

The agitated teen burst from the room and fled down the hall.

"Samantha," her mother called after her. "Don't be ridiculous. Who would ask you to stay? What are you talking about?" Peering out from the bedroom, Mrs. Jamison was horrified to see the hallway empty.

"Samantha!" Panic stabbed at her mother's heart. She raced after her daughter, searching room after room.

As she entered the blue bedroom, something caught her eye and she approached the mysterious portrait of Lord Erdely. The fuzzy image of the girl standing beside him had changed. She could almost make it out: the dress, the shoes, just like her daughter now wore. But this time she could clearly see the necklace around the girl's neck.

"This is impossible--someone's idea of a sick joke." Mrs. Jamison's eyes darted around the room. "Who is doing this? Who gave my daughter the same clothes as this picture?" Mesmerized by the portrait, she continued to stare. Parts of the blurred figure began to clear. The face remained fuzzy, but there was no mistaking the tan, beaded bracelet now visible on the figure's wrist.

"This can't be happening!" Mrs. Jamison raced from the room.

"Samantha!" she shrieked. Heads popped out from the doorways.

"Is my daughter in there? Have you seen her?"

One by one the faces disappeared as the woman frantically checked every room down the hall.

"I think I saw her, Mrs. Jamison."

"What? Where?" The distraught mother nearly knocked the short man down.

He retreated to the safety of his room.

"I'm sorry." Mrs. Jamison backed off. Gasping for breath, she tried to steady her voice. "Mr. Willows, right?"

The man nodded, looking unsure if he could trust the half-crazed woman now standing in his doorway.

"Mr. Willows, where did you see my daughter last?"

"Well, I saw her about an hour ago, having a one-sided conversation down by the little room at the end of this hallway."

"An hour ago? I've seen her since then. I need to know where she is right now!" The mother backed up to leave.

"Now hold on!" Mr. Willows held out his hand to stop her. "I just saw her again. But it was the strangest thing. I wasn't even sure she was real."

"What do you mean, not real? Of course she's real! What else—"

"No, no. You misunderstand what I'm saying. She was in that dress again, the one in the blurry portrait."

He'd seen it too!

Mr. Willows continued. "But I thought I was imagining things because she was floating down the hallway."

"Floating? What do you mean, floating?" Mrs. Jamison was barely breathing.

"I mean, there was nothing touching the ground under her dress. No feet, no legs, just the dress. And even that seemed to be disappearing."

"You're insane, Mr. Willows. Insane! How can a dress float by itself?"

"It wasn't just a dress, Mrs. Jamison. Your daughter was in it--or at least her head and arms were. But even those seemed to be vanishing." Mr. Willows glanced down the hall. "And she was definitely talking to someone—someone more invisible than she."

Mrs. Jamison trembled. She steadied herself and drew in a deep breath. "What you're describing sounds like you've seen a ghost. But my daughter is very much alive. So you could not have seen my Samantha. Ghosts are not real, Mr. Willows." Her voice rose to a piercing shrill. "Not real! Do you hear me? It was not my daughter!"

"Suit yourself." Mr. Willow pushed his door closed. "But they disappeared into the little room at the end of the hall," he whispered as the door clicked shut.

Sarina Jamison was already entering the small servant's room. She froze, trying to take in the scene before her.

"Mother?"

Her daughter's voice broke her trance.

"Samantha, who is that?"

Samantha glided back toward the tall, uniformed gentleman beside the bureau.

"You can see him? Good for you, Mom. This..." the teen took the gentleman's arm, "is Lord Erdely."

"No!" The denial came from her mother's very soul. "Don't you understand? It can't be Lord Erdely. Lord Erdely's dead. Long since dead. Centuries dead!"

"Mom, he's a..."

"Don't say it. Don't even think it. He can't be a ghost! There's no such thing as ghosts. I can see him, Samantha. If I can see him, then he's human. I don't believe in ghosts." She lowered herself to the bed as sobs wracked her body.

Samantha picked up the small portrait on the bureau and sat next to her mother.

"Look." She gently placed the picture into her mother's hands.

Her mother clumsily wiped her tears with the back of her hand. "Who is this?" she asked, sniffling.

"It's Sarah, his one true love, and her daughter. He's been waiting all these years for Sarah to return." The teen gazed up at Lord Erdely.

"And now she has."

Mrs. Jamison turned toward the voice. "What do you mean, 'now she has'? Look at this picture. The woman in this portrait is decades older than my child. Samantha is only sixteen. She has her whole life ahead of her."

"Mark the resemblance. Samantha is a descendent of my beloved Sarah. I've waited centuries for her return. I will not be denied!" Angry resolution resounded in his thunderous voice.

"It's all right, Mother. Lord Erdely loves me. He'll take care of me."

Sarina Jamison rose. As she gave the portrait back to Lord Erdely, her hand brushed against his icy cold fingers. A chill shook through her. She struggled to continue. "It's not Samantha you want. My daughter is still a child..."

Lord Erdely stared at the portrait.

Mind racing, Mrs. Jamison felt locked in a desperate battle to save her daughter, a battle she had to win. She closed her hands around Lord Erdely's, suppressing her overwhelming desire to run, to grab her child and escape this insanity. But the apparition had some kind of hold over her daughter. He was controlling everything: the portrait in the bedroom, the dress, the necklace...

Samantha's mother gasped. The necklace! Everything changed the moment her daughter had put it on. If only she could...

"Lord Erdely, if you are determined to take Samantha, may I be allowed to say good-bye? One last hug from a mother to her daughter?"

The apparition's piercing glare almost disintegrated the tiny shred of courage her mother had left. Finally, he nodded his consent.

Reaching her arms around Samantha's back, her mother drew her daughter close. "My darling," she whispered. "I know this man is true to his word. His love will last until the end of time. I will truly miss you. Despite what you think, I love you more than life itself." She gently kissed her daughter's cheek and stepped away. With one quick motion, the mother fastened the cameo necklace she had removed from the girl's neck around her own throat. She pivoted to face the menacing spirit.

"If Samantha is a descendent, then I am as well. It isn't this inexperienced child you want. Your Sarah was a woman, capable of caring for you... of..." the words caught in her throat. She swallowed and drew in a deep breath. "Of loving you. This immature little thing isn't your Sarah." Tears silently streaked down her face. "I am your Sarah!"

Samantha's thin body shook with the sudden realization of what was happening. "Mom!" shrieked the daughter, grabbing at her mother's arm. But Sarina Jamison shook her off and walked toward the ghostly figure.

Lord Erdely shifted his gaze from the young teen to the portrait, then to the mother. He reached out and touched Sarina's tears. "There is so much love in your heart for your daughter. You would sacrifice yourself for her? Your actions mirror those of my dear Sarah's. But her sacrifice took her from me. Yours brings her back to me. You are indeed my Sarah, returning after so many years."

Samantha gazed in disbelief as her lace dress was replaced with her own jeans and shirt. Glancing up she was horrified to see the dress appearing on her mother's figure, with the cameo gracefully adorning her neck.

"No! It's me you want. Don't take my mother away!"

Mrs. Jamison smiled calmly at her daughter. "It's all right, darling. Aunt Jenny will take of care you. When you get older, you can come back to the castle. I'll be here. I'll always be here for you. We both will." She took Lord Erdely's arm and the two left the small room.

It took a minute or two before Samantha shook off the horror. Then she raced to the blue bedroom.

"No!" Tears flowed down her grief-stricken face as she gazed at the portrait. Her screams brought an unwelcome intruder.

Mr. Willows popped his head into the bedroom, then made his way to Samantha's side.

"You know," he said glancing up at the large portrait on the wall. "I didn't notice it before. But the woman next to Lord Erdely in this picture sure looks a lot like your mother."

AUTHOR'S BIO:

Marcia Berneger is a freelance writer. She has stories in several anthologies (*Aleatory's Junction*, published 10/06 by Double Dragon Press, *The Healing Touch/Alzheimer's* published 5/07, and now *A Mother's Love* in The Carpathian Shadows anthology: Volume I). In addition, she is the bi-monthly Science columnist for Cecil Child Magazine and a book reviewer for myshelf.com. Additional information about her can be found on her website, www.freewebs.com/marciab

Lord Erdely's Curse
By
Charles Mossop

Part One - Transylvania: The summer of 1654

Lord John Erdely looked through the trees down a broad slope to where a young shepherd girl sat watching her flock lazily crop the thick, green grass. Several of the animals wore small brass bells and their delicate resonance drifted up the hill to where he sat astride his great black stallion, Satan. The sound mingled with the hum of bees as they busied themselves around wild rhododendron blossoms in the heat of the afternoon. The girl, aged about eighteen and wearing a white, lace-trimmed blouse and brightly colored ankle-length skirt, sang softly to herself. Lord John's eyes narrowed as he watched her and admired her comely young figure.

"I shall have her," he murmured, stroking Satan's glossy neck. "She shall be mine."

He placed his broad-brimmed hat on his head, its black ostrich plume flowing out behind. Digging his silver- spurred heels firmly into Satan's flanks, he emerged from the cover of the trees and started down the slope.

The girl looked up in alarm as she heard his approach, jumping to her feet at once.

"My lord?" she said, bobbing a quick curtsey.

"So, Magda," said Lord John, "have you thought well upon what I said?"

"Yes, my lord," she answered quietly, "and my answer must be the same. My heart is pledged to another."

"That lout Serghei Chisca?" snorted Lord John. "He is a mere boy. A bondservant. He has not two pennies to call his own. What can he possibly mean to you?"

"We were betrothed at birth." She squinted up at John in the bright sunshine, "and I love him, so please you, my lord."

"It does not please me," he answered, "it disgusts me. I, the lord of Erdely Castle, offer you fine clothes, comfort, and money to spend as you like, and you spurn and humiliate me."

The girl looked away from John for a moment, as if measuring her next words. He could see the fear in her grey eyes as she turned to him again. Satan stamped restlessly, and John tightened the reins.

"Well?" he demanded.

"Please, my lord," she said at length, tears now coursing down her cheeks, "I would wed and live in Christ's blessing with the one I love. Were I to share your bed in return for gold and precious things, I should be damned forever for my sin."

"Oh spare me your simpering piety," said John. "It is here and now that we live. If we be damned for our living after our death, then so be it."

Magda stood silent, her head bowed again, trembling.

"Your father's house is on my land, girl," said Lord John, "and your sheep crop my grass. You are my tenants and property. I could make you submit to me this very moment, here in this field."

"I know it, my lord," she said, fear plain in her voice, "but I beg you to treat me kindly, and let me be."

"I have no wish to force you, Magda," he said, less angrily. "I would have you with me of your own free will."

She looked up at him, the sun full in her face.

"It can never be so, my lord, for I love you not, nor could I ever."

"Then you are a fool." He pulled Satan around with such force the huge beast reared up on its hind legs. "I shall have you then whether you like it or not. You shall warm my bed wherever and whenever I choose, do you hear?"

The girl, dwarfed by the sheer size of the rearing stallion, shrieked in terror and dropped to her knees, hiding her face in her hands.

"Have mercy, my lord," she sobbed. "I beg of you in Christ's name."

"What has Christ to do with it?" sneered John, as Satan gathered himself for the gallop to come. "It is not Christ who will bed you, my girl, it is I."

Lord John, his swarthy face ugly with fury, spurred his mount into the trees and back along the narrow forest path in a thundering gallop. Satan foamed and glistened with sweat when John finally reined him in before a thatched stone hut on the outskirts of Cornifu. He swung down out of the saddle and strode to the rough wooden door, his high leather riding boots crunching on the gravel path.

"Toma Arcos," he shouted, beating on the door with his fist and making it rattle in its rusty iron hinges. "This is Lord John of Erdely Castle who calls. Come forth at once, for I would speak with you."

The door opened slowly, and the terrified face of a man about forty showed itself.

"How may I serve you, my lord?" the man stammered.

John reached out his hand and seized Toma's blue smock, pulling him bodily from the doorway and out into the sunshine. Toma cried out in surprise and fear.

"Now mark me well, Arcos," John said through clenched teeth. "I will have your daughter to live in Erdely Castle and be my mistress. I have told her so, but she spurns the offer. She means to marry Serghei Chisca, one of my kitchen boys: the devil take him. You will forbid the marriage, do you understand? You will forbid it, and you will order her to come to Erdely."

The mention of his daughter wrought an immediate change in Toma's demeanor. He pulled away from John's grasp and took a step backwards.

"No, my lord." He raised his chin in defiance. "I shall never do so vile a thing. Magda will marry he whom she loves, and though you break my body on your rack or roast me on a gridiron, I shall not make her a whore in your house or the house of any man, be he great or lowly."

"The rack and the gridiron?" sneered Lord John. "Don't tempt me."

John stared in rage at Toma Arcos, but he knew he was beaten—for the present. He reached up and tore down the large clove of garlic that hung on a string over the low doorway of the hut and flung it in Toma's face.

"It is not vampires you should fear, Arcos," he growled, turning back to his horse. "Fear wolves instead."

Lord John rode back to Erdely Castle, its great twin towers casting long shadows in the declining sun of early evening. It would have been simple to go to Magda's house with two or three of his retainers, seize her and bring her here, but though he burned to bed the pretty young girl, he could not bring himself to abduct and rape her. In spite of his threats, he wanted to see passion and desire in her eyes when finally he found her beside him, not fear and repulsion. He had forced many a village girl onto her back before now, and the countryside was well populated with his bastards, but Magda was different.

He walked Satan into the cobbled stable courtyard and handed the reins to a groom, then shook his head. *If she will not come to me because she wishes to, then she shall not come at all. But I swear by all the demons of darkness she and that stupid scullion of hers shall never live in peace. A curse be upon them, and upon any who seek to thwart my will. Though it take a hundred lifetimes, this curse shall not die. I shall have revenge for this humiliation.*

89

* * * *

Two nights later, Lord John, dressed in black from his hat to his boots, told his steward he was going into Cornifu. He mounted Satan and rode into the gathering dusk. After two hours he turned his horse aside and struck off through the dark forest away from the well-traveled path. He dismounted deep amongst the towering pines, and stood still. The forest vibrated with the sounds of night: owls, frogs, insects, and the animals of the dark sang and chanted a fugue of infinite variation and intricate counterpoint.

Leaving Satan loosely tethered to a bush, John walked into a narrow clearing. As he did so, the small open space immediately flooded with cold, silver radiance as the full moon sailed like a galleon from behind the clouds into the black sky above him.

He stood bathed in the light, feeling familiar stirrings within him. The transformation began. An irresistible power overwhelmed him, and he united with it as he had done so many times before. He threw back his head and roared. It was not the sound of a man's voice that echoed through the dark forest, silencing all other living things, it was the snarling roar and howl of a lone wolf on his solitary and deadly hunt. John howled again and sank to his knees. Where once there had been a man, there was now a huge, black wolf, red-eyed and white fanged.

The enormous beast looked about itself, growling, and then set off at a strong run through the purple-shadowed evergreens. Its great paws made almost no sound on the carpet of springy pine needles as it ran on steadily, its panting muzzle open and its teeth shining pale in the shafts of moonlight slanting between the tall, lowering trees.

At length, it reached the edge of the trees where it dropped into a crouch, its flanks heaving. A hundred paces away stood about thirty huts grouped around a small stone church, its lone steeple silhouetted against the night sky. The sounds of song issued from the church, carrying across the open ground to the wolf's keen ears, and they twitched as its tail thrashed angrily from side to side.

As the animal watched, unblinking, from its place of concealment in the trees, a crowd of merry-makers, some with blazing torches in hand, came out into the small open space before the church. Eight of the men carried poles on their shoulders bearing two chairs. Magda and her new husband, Serghei, sat in those chairs, laughing and singing, their hands joined. The men put the chairs down and the bride and groom knelt before the crowd, now hushed, as a black habited young priest pronounced the final prayers and benedictions of the wedding ceremony.

90

As the priest raised his hands in blessing over the young couple, the wolf emitted a malevolent howl of rage, and leaped from the trees bounding wildly toward the unsuspecting crowd of villagers.

There came a warning shout, and panic erupted everywhere. People screamed and cried to God for help. The crowd surged back toward the church, fighting for safety, and all was chaos.

Less than thirty paces from the milling crowd, the wolf let forth a yelp of pain and snapped backwards at its left flank. High on its hindquarter a stain of blood showed the feathered shaft of a small quarrel fired from a crossbow. The animal turned back toward the forest and was quickly lost from view.

The milling crowd gradually settled itself as the villagers realized the threat had passed. Thanks were offered to God, and order re-established itself.

"Whence came that shot?" called the priest, looking about him in wonder.

"It was Iuliana," cried several jubilant voices, "Iuliana Banica."

The crowd began to cheer and clap as a tall young woman approached carrying a crossbow.

"How came you by that, daughter?" asked the priest, pointing at the weapon.

"It is my brother's, Father Crainic," she announced with a smile. "I planned to use it to shoot the lucky arrow into the sky to kill the demons of darkness and bring good fortune to the bride and groom. I ran home to fetch it, and as I returned, I saw the wolf. I aimed at him, instead of the sky."

"Bless you, my child," said the priest, making the sign of the cross. "God gave you courage and you have delivered us all."

"Would that He had given me truer aim, Father," said Iuliana. "I fear the beast still lives."

"To horse," cried a young man. "We shall follow the beast's blood and finish what Iuliana so bravely started. To horse, I say."

Ten men hurried away and soon re-assembled, mounted and armed, before the church, where Father Crainic blessed them. Replacing their hats, the hunters set off, their pitch torches ruddy in the darkness.

"Begin the wedding feast," shouted one. "We shall return anon, and bring the beast's carcass with us."

The mounted men soon found the trail of blood they sought, and quickly disappeared into the trees. The wedding guests moved toward the houses, lighthearted merriment fully restored.

Homemade wine and ale flowed freely for the next two hours, and toast followed toast as the union of bride and groom was celebrated in pride and happiness. Little thought was spared for the wounded wolf as the music of violins and concertinas grew louder, and the strong drink began to take full effect.

At length the hunting party returned, weary and disheveled, and announced the wolf had not been found.

"We followed his blood," said one, gratefully accepting a flagon of dark ale, "but, of a sudden, it disappeared. We could find no trace of it. It was as though the beast had grown wings and taken flight."

"But we saw a strange thing," said another. "As we searched, we came upon the black stallion belonging to his lordship. It was saddled and had been ridden this night, I'll wager, but it bolted when we approached. His lordship was nowhere to be seen."

"*Lord John Erdely*," growled Father Crainic. "God's damnation is upon that evil man. He denies the one true Church and her rights and privilege in this land. He speaks ill of pious clergy and God-fearing laity alike. He steeps himself in the black arts and takes counsel with Beelzebub."

"Well," said the first huntsman, draining his flagon of ale and reaching for another, "whatever he was doing in the forest tonight, we saw him not."

* * * *

Two days after the wedding feast, Lord John's steward came to Cornifu to say his master had not returned home. After a further day, a search party combed the forests for hours, but no trace of him was ever found. His black stallion turned wild and roamed the pine woods incessantly, as though he, too, searched for his master. He foiled every attempt to capture him until, weeks later, he was found dead in a small clearing, emaciated and starved. The paw prints of a large wolf were found in the clearing. Those who discovered the carcass found a trail of blood leading into the forest, but as they sought to follow it, they heard a wolf howl close by, and fled for their lives.

"'Twas truly a horrible and most melancholy sound," said one.

The story of the great black wolf passed into legend, as did the name of Lord John Erdely. He became the very personification of evil, a demon incarnate. Mothers warned their children that if they were not good, Black John would catch them in their beds at midnight and eat them alive.

Magda and Serghei Chisca were both dead within two years of their marriage. Serghei died after shattering his right arm in a fall from the roof of their house, and Magda died in unspeakable agony seven months later as the abscess from a rotten tooth consumed the flesh of her face. The villagers whispered these ghastly deaths were Lord John's revenge, and Magda's father lived into old age in mortal terror of some similar fate. Iuliana Banica froze to death in a winter storm not fifty paces from the safety of her house, and it was said Lord John had lured her outside to die in the bitter cold as recompense for the pain she had inflicted upon him.

* * * *

Part Two – Cornifu, Transylvania: The summer of 2004

Margaret Archer and her father, Thomas, watched from the window of their train as the green farmland of Romania swept by. A range of mountains, not vast in scale, but rugged and steep, formed a backdrop to this unfolding panorama.

"So," said Thomas, pointing at them, "those must be the Carpathians. Yes?"

"Right," said Margaret, a woman of thirty with grey eyes and brown hair that fell in natural waves to her shoulders. "That means we're only a few hours from Cornifu. I can't wait to see Transylvania."

Her father, sitting opposite her on the long bench seat of their compartment, nodded.

"Yeah. And you know what? I'm really glad I let you talk me into making this trip. The history of this part of Europe is really fascinating."

"Now Dad," she said with a smile, "you're not going to go all Dracula on me, are you?"

"Of course not. All that vampire stuff with people living forever and sleeping in coffins is folktale and folderol."

"Maybe," Margaret said, "but many people around here still believe in it, so please don't get into any arguments, okay? I don't want people to think we're making fun of local traditions."

Thomas was about to answer when they heard the sliding door of their compartment open, and a tall, red-haired woman in her mid forties peered in.

"Do you speak English?"

"You bet," said Thomas. "Can we help you?"

"Hey," said the visitor with a smile, "Americans. May we join you? The train's really full and we can't find seats."

"Of course," said Margaret. "Come on in. I'm Margaret Archer, and this is my Dad, Thomas. We're from Detroit."

The two newcomers, each wearing jeans and carrying a backpack, entered the compartment.

"I'm Julia Baxter. I live in Los Angeles," said the redhead, heaving her pack onto the luggage rack above the seats, "and this is Steven…er…sorry, I never did get your last name."

"Chisholm," he said. "Like the trail. Detroit's my hometown, as well. Small world I guess."

There were handshakes all round and the four strangers quickly fell into relaxed conversation.

"Steven and I ran into each other at the station in Bucharest," said Julia. "We discovered we're both going to Cornifu."

"So are we," said Thomas. "Not Dracula hunting, by any chance, are you?"

"Not me," said Julia. "I really don't believe in all that."

"What about you, Steven?" asked Thomas.

"Well, as a matter of fact, I have a Master's degree in Cultural Anthropology, and I've spent a lot of time researching folktales and myths all over the world-including the Dracula stories from around here."

"But do you believe in the paranormal?" Margaret asked. "Is that why you studied it?"

"No," said Steven with an engaging grin. "I'm just very interested in the stories and folklore of people everywhere. I'm especially interested in how people use them to explain both the natural and the supernatural world. I don't believe in vampires any more than I believe in Santa Claus. They're mythical beings. One brings people gifts and is good, and the other sucks people's blood and is evil. They're both just representations."

"Well," said Margaret, "if it comes to a choice of mythical beings, I'll take Santa Claus any day."

Laughter ensued, and the talk continued amicably as the train began a slow climb into the foothills of the Carpathian Mountains. It traversed deciduous woods that gave way to pine forest, and they found themselves amongst high cliffs surmounted by jagged peaks.

"Wonderful country," said Thomas.

"It does look wild and lonely, though," said Julia, and Margaret, who had been thinking the same thing, nodded. To her, the evergreen forest, even in daylight, seemed dark and vaguely forbidding.

"We're staying at the Cornifu Hotel," said Margaret, trying to get her thoughts onto brighter subjects. "How about you?"

"I am," said Julia.

"Yep. Best place in town, I'm told," said Steven.

"According to our guidebook," said Margaret, "it's the only place in town."

"That says it all," grinned Steven.

Margaret had been watching Steven ever since he came into the compartment. She estimated his age to be close to her own and his easy and pleasant manner impressed her. She noted his fair hair, clear blue eyes, and the strong line of his jaw. She was struck with a distinct feeling she had met him before, but she could not place where or when.

About two hours after the arrival of Steven and Julia, another traveler appeared and requested a seat. Tall and strongly built, about fifty years old, he introduced himself as Bruce Campbell, from New York.

"Five Americans end up in the same train compartment in the middle of Romania," laughed Margaret.

"Must be fate," said Campbell, straight-faced.

"You don't sound like a New Yorker," said Thomas. "Bet you weren't born there."

"No, I wasn't," said Campbell, "but I live and work in Cornifu now, anyway."

"Really?" said Steven. "We're all going to stay there and see the local countryside over the next few days. Any tips?"

"That depends," answered Campbell, still stone-faced. "Are you interested in Dracula and similar stories?"

"Well," answered Steven, "I guess you could say we're all a bit intrigued by them, especially me, but none of us are committed paranormalists. We haven't come here because of Dracula or any of his friends."

"In that case," said Campbell, "I don't think there will be much for you to do in Cornifu. It's not particularly remarkable or interesting."

Strange person, thought Margaret. *I wonder if he ever smiles.*

"Oh, I'm sure there will be lots to do," said Julia brightly. "Say, why don't we all meet for dinner at the hotel tonight? The train gets in around five, so maybe dinner at seven? We can think about what we want to do."

She looked across the compartment to where Campbell sat opposite her.

"You're welcome to join us, Bruce," she said, "but, of course, you have a home to go to, don't you?"

"Thanks anyway." Campbell then lapsed into silence. For the final three hours of the journey, he said almost nothing, but sat staring fixedly out of the window.

* * * *

95

At seven o'clock that evening, Margaret, Thomas, Julia and Steven met in the dining room of the Cornifu Hotel. The room was large, old world in character, with stone walls, arched doorways and heavy, dark furniture. A large wine rack occupied almost the whole of one wall, and the Head Waiter seated them at a table close to one of the stone columns that rose to support the high ceiling.

"This is like having dinner in a castle," said Thomas, looking around.

Halfway through the meal, Margaret caught sight of a pretty brunette in her early thirties entering the dining room. She stood for a moment, scanning the room, and Margaret found herself hoping Steven wouldn't notice how attractive she was. The brunette, however, made straight for their table.

"I'm sorry to interrupt," she said, smiling. "My name is Jennifer Brooks, and I'd like to give you this letter."

She handed sealed envelopes to each of them, and wishing them a pleasant evening, left the dining room.

Margaret tore open the envelope and quickly read the contents.

"It's from that guy on the train, Bruce Campbell."

The American Paranormal Association of World Tours," said Julia. "That's a weird name. Doesn't make sense. Is it a company, an association, or what?"

"Who knows," said Thomas, "but this Campbell fella is inviting us on a free trip tomorrow. All expenses paid."

"To Erdely Castle, no less," said Margaret. "I've read about that place."

"Me too," said Steven. "It's a fine example of seventeenth century castle construction, and it's been very carefully restored over the past few years."

"No kidding," said Thomas. "Are you saying you're interested in going on this junket?"

"Why not, Dad?" asked Margaret. "It would be a great way to see the local area, and a genuine piece of Transylvanian history."

"And all for free," added Julia. "I'm in."

"Me too," said Steven. "It's probably nothing more than a promotional thing for Campbell's company, but it could be fun."

"Well, I'm not sure," said Thomas. "I mean, we don't know anything about this American Paranormal whatever-it-is. If they're into the paranormal stuff, they might all be prize-winning weirdoes, and I'm not sure I trust that Campbell fella, anyway. He didn't say much, just sat there like a spare part with a blank look on his face."

"I wouldn't worry, Thomas," Steven said, and Margaret heard the clear note of confidence in his voice.

"It just doesn't feel right somehow," Thomas said to Margaret.

"There's four of us," said Steven, "and we can look after ourselves. I say let's go have a look at Erdely Castle."

Thomas reluctantly gave in.

"Okay. You win. We'll go. But something still feels strange to me. I hope Campbell doesn't come with us, he was beginning to give me the creeps by the time we got here."

* * * *

The following morning, under an overcast sky, Margaret, her father, Julia and Steven met outside the hotel. At eight-thirty, a dark blue minivan drew up to the curb and Jennifer Brooks alighted. She wore a white blouse and dark slacks, and Margaret noticed Steven eying her appreciatively.

"Hi there," said Jennifer brightly. "I'm so glad you all decided to come."

Bruce Campbell, who appeared a moment later, shook hands all round and wished them a good trip.

"Thanks," said Steven. "It's a little unexpected. Very generous of you, though."

"I'm glad to be able to do it." Campbell's smile had no warmth, and struck Margaret as faintly mocking.

They boarded the van, and as they drew out into the traffic Margaret saw Campbell turn and walk away. He seemed to have a slight limp.

Jennifer turned to face them from the front passenger seat.

"Our driver's name is Vlad," she said. "He can neither hear nor speak, but he's an excellent driver, and he'll look after us very well, I assure you."

"Let's hope so," said Thomas to Margaret, quietly. "I'm not big on drivers who can't hear anything."

The van left the winding streets and tall, narrow houses of Cornifu, and passed through long stretches of green, upland pastures before climbing further into the mountains. At noon, they stopped by a fast-flowing river whose white water foamed and leaped around large granite boulders. In spite of increasing clouds, the weather remained pleasantly warm and Margaret found the mountain air sweet and invigorating.

"Time for a bite," Jennifer said.

Steven chuckled. "I thought that sort of thing only happened at midnight."

"Of lunch," she answered with a laugh.

Jennifer and Vlad spread lunch on the van's tailgate and everyone helped themselves to cold chicken lightly seasoned with paprika, fresh rolls and hot coffee from a thermos. Sitting on the bank of the rushing stream on folding chairs Vlad produced from the back of the van, they ate while Jennifer told them about Erdely Castle.

"The locals swear it's haunted. I wouldn't be surprised if it was, but the stories all go back to Lord John Erdely."

"I read about him," said Margaret, through a mouthful of cold chicken. "Seventeenth century, wasn't he?"

"Yes. He died, or rather disappeared, in the summer of 1654. He isn't a Dracula, or vampire, figure, but there are local legends that say he could turn himself into a wolf. His interest in the black arts is a matter of historical record, though. In fact, at one point he was on the verge of being excommunicated after openly defying a Bishop's order to stop what the Church called his *devil worship*."

"I'll bet," put in Steven. "The black arts weren't big with the Church in the seventeenth century."

"They have such happy stories in these parts," said Thomas.

"How is it you know so much about this, Jennifer?" asked Julia.

"I have a degree in Romanian history and literature from the University of Bucharest," she said. "I originally came here on an exchange from UCLA, but by the time the exchange semester was finished I'd fallen in love with Romania, so I stayed and finished my degree. After graduation I met Bruce, and he was in need of a bilingual guide. I fit the bill, and the rest is history, as they say."

"Back to Lord John for a minute," said Steven. "If he isn't a Dracula figure, then what is he?"

"He's more of a haunting, evil presence, but his sort of evil spirit doesn't just go about the countryside at night scaring the you-know-what out of people. Even today it's still believed spirits like his can interfere in the lives of living people and do them harm. Can lay curses on them and so forth."

"So Lord John could still be wandering around his castle terrifying unsuspecting tourists," said Steven, grinning.

"Could be," said Jennifer, "although there's never been a sighting…so far."

"You say such beliefs are still held today?" said Thomas.

"Yes. Many of the old beliefs persist in these parts. For example, some people still hang a clove of garlic over their front door to ward off vampires. They've done it for centuries."

"Fascinating," said Margaret.

"Well," Jennifer said, getting to her feet, "it's time we got underway again."

Everyone lent a hand to pack up, and they set off once again. Thomas sat beside Margaret, and she noticed he seemed unusually somber and withdrawn.

"You okay, Dad?" she asked quietly.

"I guess," Thomas replied. "More and more I wish I wasn't here. It feels dangerous or something. I don't know…"

"I think," Margaret said, squeezing his arm affectionately, "you've just got a touch of culture shock. Don't worry, Dad. Everything's fine."

An hour later the winding road emerged from the pine forest onto a broad, sparsely treed plateau. In the distance, its towers and battlements looking cold and forbidding, stood the black bulk of Erdely Castle. Rain had begun to fall shortly after lunch and, for Margaret, it added an atmosphere of bleak loneliness to the place.

"Not a very welcoming sight, is it?" said Thomas as they pulled up before the great wrought iron gates set in the high stone wall surrounding the castle.

"Look at the pattern on those gates," said Julia. "There's three crosses on each one, but they're all upside down."

"It's a sign of Satan worship," said Steven. "The inverted crosses point downwards towards Hades. They symbolize the superiority of Mephistopheles over Christ. The triumph of evil over good."

"No wonder the Church didn't like Lord John," said Margaret. "He and Faust would have got on well together."

Jennifer jumped out and opened the gates and Vlad drove into the castle grounds and stopped. The ponderous gates closed behind them with a loud clank, and Jennifer ran back to the van.

"Ugh," she said, as they moved off again, "it would rain. But don't worry, gang, everything we want to see is inside."

"I hope so," said Margaret. "These gardens are completely overgrown and gone wild."

"There's no landscape work done," explained Jennifer, "but the building itself has to be properly maintained because Romania has declared it a historic site. Our company sends a small crew in here several times a month and they check everything, and also stock the kitchen. We'll take a short rest before we tour the castle. After that, we'll have some light refreshments and then head back to Cornifu. We should be back at the hotel just after dark."

"Can't be soon enough for me," muttered Thomas, but only Margaret heard him.

Margaret was enthralled by the castle, which had been filled with seventeenth century antique furniture and fittings: upholstered wooden benches, capacious chairs, and wood floors shining with rubbed beeswax. Heavy tapestries adorned the stone walls of the main rooms depicting hunting parties pursuing deer and wild boar, and scenes from classical mythology with nymphs, satyrs and centaurs cavorting in idyllic Arcadian fields.

As she admired the castle, however, Margaret kept a watchful eye on her father, who appeared to be increasingly uncomfortable and nervous. He continually looked over his shoulder as if afraid something or someone was following them. She asked him if he was all right, but he shook his head and said nothing.

They walked through a vast dining hall down whose center ran an immense and highly polished wooden table with twenty chairs ranged on each side, and then down a wide corridor. Just before entering the kitchen they came to a strip of bare ground with small stones and pebbles that unexpectedly cut through the flagstones of the passageway.

"This looks like a dry streambed," said Julia.

"Got it in one," said Steven. "This was a stream in Lord John's time. The servants had to walk through it to make sure their feet were clean before they entered the dining hall."

"That's quite right," said Jennifer. "How did you know that?"

"I'm not exactly sure," answered Steven. "I just sort of knew it. I guess I must have read about it somewhere or other."

They sat around a small table in the kitchen and had snacks of bread and strong cheese, cake and more coffee, and as they finished, Jennifer's cell phone rang. She retrieved it from her purse, excused herself, and went out.

"I'm glad they put electricity in the kitchen," said Julia. "The fresh hot coffee was very welcome."

"I wonder if there's electricity anywhere else in the place," said Steven, and Margaret shook her head.

"I don't think so. I didn't see any switches or sockets or anything."

"Nor did I," said Julia, as Jennifer returned, a somber look on her face.

"Bad news I'm afraid, folks," she said, sitting down again. "This has never happened before, but I'm afraid we're sort of stuck here."

"Stuck?" said Thomas, alarm in his voice. "What do you mean?"

"I mean stuck. That was Bruce on the phone. Apparently the rain we had here was much heavier lower down, and it washed the road out."

"Surely there's another way back," said Thomas, and Jennifer shook her head.

"I'm afraid not."

"Terrific," said Thomas, looking around the table at the others. "I knew something like this would happen. I told you I had a bad feeling about this, didn't I?"

"Come on Dad," said Margaret, "It's not that bad. After all, where else would you get a chance to spend a night in a seventeenth century castle?"

"Who said I wanted to?"

Thomas looked around the kitchen, his face pale, his fingers drumming nervously on the table.

"We'll be all right," Jennifer put in, "and you'll find everything you need in the bedrooms. We planned for this kind of emergency, so there's nothing to worry about. There's plenty of food in the fridge as well. I'm sorry for the inconvenience to everyone, but..."

"Okay then," said Steven, "that's it I guess. It's not your fault Jennifer."

"We'll make the best of it," added Julia. "It'll be like camping."

Steven prepared dinner, and Margaret found she was not at all surprised that he was a good cook. Somehow, she almost expected it. The feeling that she had seen him before simply would not go away, and now she felt a growing sense of understanding between them, an indefinable consciousness of familiarity.

"Great food, Steven." said Julia.

"Thanks. I sort of feel I know my way around this kitchen somehow. God knows why."

"Well, *I* don't feel at home in it," muttered Thomas, who had not touched a scrap of his meal.

"By the way," said Steven, "where's Vlad?"

"He has his own room," said Jennifer. "He prefers not to be around people if he can help it."

When darkness approached, candles were issued to all, and Jennifer showed them to their respective bedrooms. Walking through the lonely passageways of Erdely Castle with the candles casting disembodied shadows on the stone walls, Margaret experienced a strange feeling of oppression, a troubled foreboding, as if some malevolent entity accompanied them all as they walked.

"This is a bit creepy," she whispered to Steven, and he put his arm around her shoulders for a moment and gave her a quick squeeze.

"This day trip is turning out to be a lot more than we expected," he said, "but there's nothing to be frightened of."

As they passed a large mullioned window Julia looked out and abruptly stopped.

"Look at that. Did you ever see a full moon like that before?"

The clouds had thinned a little. As they stood staring at the huge silver orb suspended motionless in the dark purple sky, Thomas spoke, breaking the silence unexpectedly.

"I think I'll go out for a breath of fresh air before I turn in. This place is really getting on my nerves."

"Good God," said Julia, "you can't go outside now. It's freezing."

"Hardly," said Thomas, with a short laugh. "It's the middle of summer."

"I'll come with you," said Margaret. "You shouldn't go out alone."

"Don't bother. I'll be fine."

"Just don't get lost," Jennifer called after him, but Thomas had already disappeared around a corner and did not reply.

"Is he a bit claustrophobic, Margaret?" asked Jennifer.

"Not at all, but he's been acting strangely ever since you told us we'd have to stay."

"Well, once everyone's sorted out I'll go and find him," said Jennifer. "I think he'll probably be all right once he has a chance to settle down and rest."

Margaret remained worried, but once again Steven reassured her. She found his presence comforting, his words confident, and she could still feel the strength of his arm around her shoulders although it was no longer there.

"Thomas told me he heard a wolf howl while we were at dinner," said Julia, as they moved off again. "I meant to mention it before, but it slipped my mind. I didn't hear anything myself."

"A wolf?" echoed Margaret.

"It couldn't be, really," Jennifer said. "There are no wolves left in this part of the Carpathians. They were hunted out at least a hundred years ago, if not more."

Jennifer showed everyone to their rooms, and then told Margaret she would go and bring Thomas back inside.

"He won't know which room is his otherwise," she pointed out.

Margaret was given a large room, well furnished with antiques. The bed was clean and comfortable, necessary toiletries were provided and there was a small washbasin in one corner as a concession to modern convenience.

She blew out the candle and settled herself, but sleep eluded her until, about ten minutes later, there came a soft tap on the door and a voice from the corridor.

"Margaret, it's Jennifer. Your father's fine. He's safe in his room. Good night."

"Thanks. Good night."

Relieved at the news, Margaret closed her eyes, but as she slid into sleep she suddenly found herself sitting upright in bed, wide awake. A mournful, far-off sound had reached her. An ethereal cadence that seemed to float and hover on the night air. A strangely familiar sound. A wolf. As she lay back slowly, Margaret felt ill-at-ease and troubled. She slept only fitfully.

* * * *

Margaret awoke the following morning feeling neither rested nor refreshed. She looked out of her bedroom window and saw a gray and cloudy sky. The memory of the wolf's chilling howl sent a shiver through her, and she hoped the road had been repaired so they could all leave this oppressive and unsettling place.

She descended the wide main staircase and found her way to the kitchen where Jennifer was preparing breakfast.

"Good morning," said Jennifer. "Sleep well?"

"Not really. I heard a wolf last night."

'You were probably dreaming." Jennifer smiled.

"No, I wasn't. I heard it quite clearly."

"It can't have been a wolf." Jennifer put on the coffee.

"Well it sure sounded like one. It gave me the creeps."

She helped Jennifer set out breakfast, and soon Steven and Julia appeared. Neither had heard the wolf, so Margaret decided to drop the subject.

"Where's Thomas?" asked Julia.

"I'll go roust him out." After only a few minutes, though, Steven returned to the kitchen and Margaret immediately sensed something was wrong.

"What is it?"

"Your father isn't in his room, and his bed hasn't been slept in."

"*What?*" said Jennifer, alarm on her face. "I left him in his room last night, and he said he was going to bed."

"Well, he obviously didn't," said Steven. "Did anyone hear him leave his room? Go down the corridor? Anything?"

"Something's happened to him." Margaret felt fear's cold fingers clutch her stomach.

"I'm sure there's an ex…" began Jennifer, but Vlad's unexpected appearance cut her short. The driver's eyes bulged and his face was chalk white. Beckoning frantically at them, he turned and made for the back entrance.

The four hurried after him, Margaret's heart pounding as though it would break her ribs.

Vlad led them outside into the overgrown kitchen garden and pointed with a trembling finger.

Thomas's body lay face down in a tangle of brambles and weeds in what had once been a vegetable bed.

"Dad," Margaret screamed, and ran forward, pushing past Steven as he attempted to hold her back.

She dropped to her knees beside her father's inert form, sick with dread and horror. She rolled him onto his back.

Thomas's lifeless face, wet with dew, stared up at her, ghostly pale, wide-eyed, and contorted in a rictus of terror. Below his chin a bloody, gaping wound showed that his throat had been torn out.

Margaret felt the world collapse on her. Her senses tumbled into a spinning vortex that carried her down into darkness as she struggled to breathe.

She had no recollection of returning to the kitchen, or how long she had been unconscious, but eventually she found herself sitting at the table, a cup of coffee before her. She stared at it, her eyes fixed and unseeing, stunned and numb.

She uttered no protest as Jennifer and Julia took her upstairs to her room and gently helped her onto the bed. She had a dim aware of Julia giving her a pill and a glass of water.

"Here, Margaret. This'll make you sleep."

She drank down the small tablet and merciful, all-obliterating sleep overcame her.

* * * *

When she awoke, Margaret felt as if someone had stuffed her head with thick wool. She couldn't think.

Memory burst into her consciousness like the waters of a breaking dam, and she lay trembling, tears running down her cheeks from under tightly closed eyelids.

A half hour later, she got up and washed her face at the small washbasin. She glanced at her watch. Three o'clock. She had been asleep for most of the day. She now found she wanted to be with the others, she craved company, and she needed Steven's company most of all. She

104

noticed a dull pain had appeared in her mouth. A toothache, she thought, although she'd been to the dentist quite recently.

Margaret left her room and went along the stone-sided passageway to the main staircase, which swept in an enormous arc down to the ground floor. She reached the flag stoned foyer at the foot of the stairs and then walked to one of the large floor-to-ceiling mullioned windows that afforded a view of the grounds between the castle and its surrounding wall. She glanced out across the untended lawn and then staggered backwards with a piercing scream as a huge form leaped up outside the window. For a hideous instant she stood staring into the face of a great black wolf, its red eyes burning like coals in a fire. Its slavering, white fanged jaws snapped at her before it leaped aside and disappeared.

* * * *

Steven waited for Julia and Jennifer in the kitchen and gave them each a cup of strong coffee.

"How is she?" he asked, aware that he was desperately worried about her.

"Sleeping, poor girl," said Julia. "I gave her one of my pills. They'd conk out an elephant."

"This is awful," said Jennifer. "I tried to call Bruce, but he's not answering his cell or his phone at the office."

"Can't you call the police?" asked Julia. "Surely we ought to be telling somebody what's happened."

"I tried, but I couldn't get through. The connection was really awful. They couldn't hear me at all."

"That's too bad," said Steven. "They could tell us about the road as well."

"I guess the only thing I can do is keep trying Bruce," said Jennifer. "His line seemed clear, but he just didn't answer."

There was a short silence before Steven spoke again.

"A trail of blood led away from Thomas's body, and it sure as hell couldn't have been his. He died where he fell."

"It must have been a wild dog or something," said Julia.

"Well," said Steven, draining his cup of coffee, "whatever it was, it must have been pretty damn big, and it caught Thomas by surprise. There's no indication of a struggle. No smaller bite wounds or scratches. Just that one giant bite to the throat."

"Why in God's name did he go back outside?" said Jennifer.

"Who knows?" said Steven, "but he was certainly worried about something when we all went to bed last night."

"Where is Thomas now?" asked Jennifer.

105

"We put him in a storage room near the back entrance," said Steven. "Vlad found a blanket to cover him with."

Julia complained she felt cold and told them she thought it perhaps signaled the onset of what she called one of her *famous migraines*.

"I think I'll go take a pill myself and see if I can sleep it off."

"Are you sure Margaret's all right?" Steven asked after Julia went upstairs.

"She's sound asleep," said Jennifer from the sink where she was rinsing the coffee cups. "It's the best thing for her right now."

"Yeah, I guess so..."

"I just don't know why Thomas would have gone outside again. Why would he do that?"

Steven hardly heard Jennifer. He stared down at the wooden tabletop thinking about Margaret. He felt strongly attracted to her, but not simply as an ephemeral holiday romance or casual bed partner. There was much more to it than that. He could not shake the thought that he knew her from somewhere; that he had met her before. He remembered putting his arm around her the previous evening in the corridor, and recalled how natural and familiar a gesture it had been. As if he had done it many times before. But that was not possible; they had only met the day before yesterday...or had they? He could not get his head around it all. He stood, feeling a need to be active.

"Look, Jennifer," he said, "I'm not very good at sitting still, especially at times like this. Can I go exploring a bit? Castles like this always have major networks of dungeons and storage cellars. I'm sure there's a way to get down into them here."

"Sure," said Jennifer. "They're interesting. There's some old torture stuff down there, and a load of old weapons. We've been trying to get someone to do a proper inventory and appraisal of it all."

She took a bunch of keys from her pocket and, prying one off, tossed it over to him.

"There you go. That'll get you through the door that leads to the cellar stairs. It's just to the left of the main front door. Enjoy yourself."

"Thanks," Steven said, pocketing the key. "Will you be okay by yourself?"

"Of course. Go on."

Steven moved to the archway that led from the kitchen toward the great dining hall, and then stopped.

"What do I do for light down there?"

"There's a switch at the head of the stairs. The cellar's the only other place with electricity aside from the kitchen, but it's still not great."

106

"I'll manage."

Within a few minutes Steven had unlocked the cellar door and starting down the stairs. The light was not at all good, but it was sufficient, and when he reached the bottom of the stairs he found himself in a cavernous space built entirely of stone, its ceiling supported by columns whose capitals spread out into an intersecting fan pattern above his head. The air felt cool and moist. Everything was profoundly still. Apart from the sound of his own breathing, he heard absolutely nothing. He looked slowly around.

But—and he frowned—this was not new to him. He had been here before surely. The sight of this area stirred a distant but unmistakable memory. Yes. The casks of wine and brandy were kept here in Lord John's day.

Smaller rooms led off from this large main gallery, many of them sealed by heavy wooden doors.

"Storage rooms," he said aloud, his voice returning to him from the unyielding stone around him. "That's right."

These fleeting recollections puzzled Steven, but he dismissed them as tricks of *déjà vu,* such as are experienced by everyone from time to time. They meant nothing.

He walked down a narrow passageway and found himself in the castle's dungeons. The cells had lost their barred doors over the centuries, but each contained what looked like dusty pieces of old machinery. Upon closer inspection, Steven recognized them as medieval instruments of torture. He stared at a wicked-looking device with chains, ratchets and pulleys on it, and in the gloomy half-light he could picture the scene of centuries ago. Flaming torches set in sconces on the walls, branding irons brought to red heat amongst glowing coals and the agonized screams of the tormented echoing down the long stone passageways. A glimpse into hell. He found it so easy to imagine. As if he had actually seen it. He lingered, lost in this reverie.

"Christ!" Steven yelled as powerful hands gripped him from behind. He struggled to free himself. A man shouted at him, but he couldn't understand a word. Wrenching himself loose, he darted into the passage and then turned to face his assailant.

"Who the hell are you?" he demanded.

A human-like apparition confronted him: the figure of a tall man dressed in black breeches and a black coat. He wore a broad-brimmed hat adorned with a black ostrich plume. Glittering garnet-red eyes accentuated his swarthy features.

The spectral vision seemed insubstantial, but its strength was real enough. Steven sidestepped as the figure lunged at him again, but stumbled over some unseen object and lost his balance. The man seized him in a numbing grip and dragged him toward a rack in a nearby cell. Steven felt himself being forced down onto the machine and knew if even one of his wrists were chained, he would have no hope of escape. With all the strength his desperation and fear bestowed on him, he kicked himself away from the rack, momentarily breaking the specter's hold.

Steven dashed away again, but misjudged his direction and found himself trapped face to face with a solid stone wall. Dry-mouthed with fear, his heart hammering in his chest, and his right arm aching, Steven turned to face his attacker.

As the figure advanced, red eyes glowing malevolently, Steven caught sight of a heavy table on his right piled high with what looked like pieces of rusty metal. Seizing one of them, he discovered it was a long-bladed dagger.

The apparition moved toward him, still talking in low, menacing tones, and Steven caught a glimpse of a bloodstain darkening the breeches on its left thigh. He brandished the dagger at the advancing figure, and to his surprise, a look of fear crossed its face and it stood still.

Quickly realizing what might be happening, Steven glanced at the dagger and saw it had a plain hilt, making the weapon resemble a cross. He grasped it by the blade and shook it at the figure. It retreated a step. Steven advanced, and with a shriek of rage, the apparition vanished from sight.

Steven, breathless and trembling, and now alone in the dimly lit passageway, heard the dagger clatter onto the stone floor as it fell from his nerveless fingers. He turned and ran back into the main gallery and up the stairs, two at a time.

He burst into the entrance hall and, slamming the cellar door behind him, ran through the dining hall toward the kitchen.

Jennifer sat reading at the table when Steven stumbled into the kitchen, and jumped to her feet in alarm, tipping her chair over behind her with a loud crash. She stared at him, wide-eyed.

"*Steven?* What...?"

"My God, Jennifer," he gasped, and sank down onto a chair.

Recovering herself, Jennifer gave him a shot of scotch.

After a time, he managed to tell her what had happened.

She shook her head in disbelief, but grew ashen-faced as he described the apparition he had seen.

"Finish that drink and come with me," she said.

Steven followed her along a series of hallways, and then, unlocking another door, she ushered him into a vast space lined from floor to ceiling with carved wooden shelves filled with books. Steven smelled the musty odor of old leather and binder's glue as he looked around the room.

"We didn't see this on our tour," he said.

"No," said Jennifer. "We don't include it any more, since we lost several old volumes to light-fingered visitors. It seemed better to just close it up."

"There must be thousands of books here," said Steven.

"Nearly seven thousand, actually, but it's not them I want you to see." She pointed to Steven's left. "It's that over there."

Daylight streamed in through two large windows, and in a niche on the wall opposite them, he saw a large oil painting in an ornately carved gilt frame-a portrait of a swarthy-featured man, wearing dark clothes and a hat with a black ostrich plume.

"My God," he said, after calming his churning stomach. "That's him."

"It's Lord John Erdely. I'd almost forgotten that painting was here, but I saw it when I came to get a book to read after you went down into the cellars."

As he stared at the painting, the rational, intellectual side of Steven's mind battled with the memory of his experience in the cellars. The sight of the painting set him in turmoil. He shook his head and made a small noise of exasperation with his tongue.

"But, look," he said at length. "It still could have been some idiot trying to frighten us for some stupid reason. I mean, anyone could dress up to look like Lord John."

"Yes, but could anyone just disappear the way you described?"

Steven was silent, recalling the chilling sound made by the apparition as it vanished. No human trickster could have done that.

"And don't forget," Jennifer went on, "Margaret's father was killed by an animal, and the local stories say Lord John could turn himself into a wolf. And Margaret told me she heard a wolf last night."

Steven felt forced into believing in things he once thought to be utterly impossible.

"Jennifer, are you saying all this is real? That Lord John's ghost, or spirit, or whatever the hell it was, is wandering around here?"

"I'm not sure," she answered, "but you're the one who saw it. And from the way you looked when you came back upstairs, I'd say whatever you saw must have been pretty real."

"It was real." He examined the bruises on his arm where the vision had grabbed him. "It got hold of me, and I fought with it. I didn't imagine it."

"I never thought you did. There may well be something here beyond our understanding."

"It's bizarre, but I think you're probably right. I…"

A shrill scream echoed through the room, and Steven froze.

"That came from the entrance hall I think," said Jennifer, but Steven was already running.

"It's Margaret."

They found her lying on her back on the slate floor of the hallway, sobbing and trembling. She clung to Steven as he knelt beside her, holding her tightly.

"It's all right," he reassured her. "It's all right. What was it? What happened?"

"A wolf," she sobbed. "There, at that window. It just appeared out of nowhere. It had horrible red eyes."

He looked up at Jennifer, who nodded.

"That's what the legend says. A red-eyed wolf."

Steven helped Margaret to her feet, and asked Jennifer to take her into the kitchen and stay with her.

"Give her a shot of that scotch," he said. "I'm going to see if there's any trace of a wolf out there."

"No, Steven," cried Margaret. "Don't."

"Be still," he said. "I'll be all right. Go with Jennifer."

Be still, he thought in surprise as he went towards the front door. Where had that come from? He had never used the expression in his life before.

* * * *

Julia awoke to the sound of a scream from somewhere in the castle, and lay for a moment trying to collect her fuzzy thoughts together. The pain of her migraine was gone, but the powerful sleeping pills always left her groggy.

Very slowly she got up off her bed and went along the corridor to the top of the staircase. She descended, and went along to the kitchen where she found Margaret and Jennifer. Margaret, waxen-faced, held a small glass of what looked like whiskey in a trembling hand, and Jennifer was busy with her cell phone.

110

"Are you absolutely sure, Bruce?" Jennifer asked, and paused for the answer. "Okay. If that's the way it is, it'll have to do, I guess. Thanks. Bye."

"I thought I heard a scream," said Julia, helping herself to coffee. "What's going on?"

"Well," said Jennifer, drawing a deep breath, "I know what's happened, but I don't think anyone knows what's going on."

"And what's that supposed to mean?"

"Steven's been attacked by what appears to be Lord John Erdely's ghost in the cellars, and Margaret's just seen a red-eyed wolf outside the window."

"Good God. That's absurd."

"Absurd it may be," said Steven, coming into the kitchen, "but I know what I saw, and there's a blood trail outside the window just like the one that led away from Thomas's body."

Julia looked at the other three and tried to understand what she was hearing. Margaret's father had been killed, but not by a wolf. A wild dog, maybe, but not a wolf.

"You said there were no wolves left," said Julia, "and even if there were, no wolf would come that close to the castle. I mean…how would it get over the wall?"

"This doesn't seem to be an ordinary wolf."

"It was horrible," said Margaret, and Steven went and sat beside her.

"Be still," he said, "we're safe in here."

"Safe from what?" Julia said. "I have no idea what this is all about. Wolves with red eyes? Ghosts in the cellar? This is all nonsense. There's some rational explanation for it all. These things you're talking about just don't exist."

"Can't we just go?" said Margaret.

"I'm afraid not," Jennifer replied. "I finally got in touch with Bruce and he says the road is still out. They have assured him it will be repaired by mid-morning tomorrow."

"I won't stay another night," Margaret declared. "I can't, I just can't."

"We can't go anywhere else, Margaret," Jennifer said. "God knows I wish we could, but you remember the road we came up. There's nothing there, not even a farmhouse, until we get out of the mountains. And we can't do that until tomorrow morning."

"Look," said Steven. "I suggest we all stay together tonight. There are twin beds in my room, a sofa, and a big chair. I'll take the chair; I doubt I'll sleep anyway."

Julia didn't believe the ghost stories, and had never liked sharing rooms with people.

"Thanks anyway, Steven, but I'm sure I'll be just fine. Besides, it's so damn cold in this place, I've had the oil heater on in my room all day. I'm still cold. I'd much rather stay in my own warm room."

"Cold?" said Jennifer.

"Aren't you cold?" Julia asked. "I'm freezing. I wish I'd brought a thick sweater, or even a good jacket."

"It's not cold at all," protested Steven. "We're not that high up in the mountains."

"Well," said Julia, "I'm feeling colder all the time now. Even just standing here."

Jennifer took hold of Julia's hand.

"You feel absolutely frozen."

"Told you."

Margaret rubbed the side of her face gingerly.

"This toothache's getting worse," she complained. "That's all I need."

They ate a quick supper and Jennifer took a note to Vlad telling him they would leave in the morning.

"How is he?" asked Steven, when she returned.

"Fine," she answered. "He's still in his own little room at the back, oblivious to everything, buried in a spy novel. I didn't tell him anything."

"He'll be okay," said Julia. "None of this has anything to do with him, or you, Jennifer."

"What do you mean?" asked Steven.

Julia hesitated, frowning. Her words had surprised even her.

"I'm not sure," she said. "It's just a feeling, I guess."

But she knew it was far more than that. She felt certain that whatever was taking place in this old castle concerned only the three of them. She pushed the matter from her thoughts and reminded herself she didn't believe any of it.

As night closed its black hand around the gaunt and brooding towers of Erdely Castle, Margaret, Steven, Julia and Jennifer went, candles in hand, up the carved staircase to their rooms. Jennifer had also declared she would stay by herself, and took her book with her into her room, but Margaret insisted she would not be alone.

* * * *

Margaret went into Steven's room and lay down on one of the beds while Steven took the other. Sleep was impossible. They left a candle burning on the night table between the beds, and Margaret lay in the pale

112

orange light, staring at the ceiling. She thought of her father, and the terrifying image of the red-eyed wolf rose unbidden in her mind. She trembled in an agony of grief and monumental fear.

"Steven," she called. "Are you asleep?"

"Fat chance."

"I'm so terribly frightened."

He rolled off his bed and slipped onto hers, taking her into his arms.

"The wolf is still here," she said, her face buried in his shoulder. "I know it is. I can feel it."

"Go to sleep," he said. "It'll all be over in the morning."

In spite of herself, Margaret laughed softly.

"That's what you always used to say when I was afraid of thunderstorms."

"Yes," he said. "Don't ask me how, Margaret, but I'm certain you and I were together once. Somewhere. Sometime. And I loved you."

"And I loved you, too," she said. "That feeling has been growing in me ever since I first saw you on the train from Bucharest."

She snuggled closer to him, and he grunted.

"My right arm is killing me," he said. "It's really sore."

"Like my tooth," she said. "My face is starting to swell, I think. It must be an abscess, but it's come on really quickly."

"I wonder..." Steven began, but he was silenced by a choking cry from down the passageway.

* * * *

Julia, shivering with cold, went into her room and was relieved to feel the warmth of the oil heater. Why was she so damn cold? She lay down, fully clothed, on the bed, and pulled the thick eiderdown over herself. She had no thought of sleep, but gradually, her mind dulled by the numbing cold that had come over her again in spite of the heater, she drifted into a state of half-slumber.

Slowly, through the mist of her confused consciousness, she became aware of a strange sound outside her bedroom door. It reminded her of a dog, snuffling and clawing. Not loud, but unmistakable.

She sat up. The sound stopped. She lay back, and it resumed.

Scratching. Sniffing.

"Damn it," she said under her breath, and searched for the matches on the small table by the bed. "What now?"

Lighting the candle, she got up and went to the door.

The sound ceased, and Julia hesitated.

The sound returned.

She turned the key in the lock, and pulled open the door. A great red-eyed apparition in the form of a black wolf leaped at her and bore her to the floor. She screamed for an instant before she felt the creature's fangs sink into her neck. There was a moment of horrific pain, a frantic struggle for breath, and then oblivion.

* * * *

"What the hell was that?" said Steven, getting to his feet. "Was that Julia?"

"Wait," called Margaret, as he strode toward the door. "Don't leave me alone. I'm coming too."

She and Steven came out into the hall, nearly colliding with Jennifer as she emerged from her own room, and the three of them hurried down the passage toward the faint glow of candlelight from Julia's open doorway.

They found Julia lying just inside her bedroom, blood spreading onto the wooden floor from a gaping gash where her throat had been.

"Oh God," breathed Jennifer.

Steven knelt and took Julia's wrist.

"No pulse," he said. "Hardly surprising."

"What are we going to do?" said Margaret, shaking with fear and repulsion.

"And there's the trail of blood again," said Steven, pointing along the hallway.

They slid Julia's body further into her room, closed the door and the three of them walked quickly back to Steven's room. They locked the door, lit all the candles they could find, and sat awake until sunrise. Margaret huddled against Steven as he sat with his left arm around her shoulders.

"Your face is quite swollen, Margaret," said Jennifer at one point, and Margaret nodded.

"It's getting really painful now," she said.

"So is my arm," said Steven. "It almost feels like it's broken, but I know it's not."

"God," said Jennifer, "I just thought of something. Assuming it was Erdely's ghost that attacked you downstairs, he…it…could get in here easily."

"Don't worry," said Steven. "There's actually no chance he'll even try it. Look over the bed. I hadn't noticed it before.""

They saw a small wooden crucifix hanging on the wall.

"He won't come anywhere near a cross," said Steven, "and if one actually touched him, he'd be finished for good."

* * * *

Morning arrived with a cloudless sky and the three of them went down to the kitchen, Steven carrying the crucifix he had taken from the bedroom wall. Jennifer wrote a hasty note to Vlad about Julia, and the driver stared at it, appalled. White-faced, he helped Steven load the two bodies into the van.

Without thought of breakfast, they left Erdely Castle as quickly as they could. Jennifer unlocked the gates and Vlad, his face still a mask of shock and horror, sped them down the mountain road toward Cornifu.

Margaret held Steven's hand as they sat together in the back seat, thinking of her father lying behind her, and wishing desperately she had never come up with the idea of visiting Romania. She wanted the nightmare to be over, and it was only after an hour's driving that her heart calmed and she felt her terror begin to subside.

Her thoughts turned to Steven and what he had said to comfort her the previous night. She had heard him speak those words so many times before. Somewhere. And why were they both now convinced they had known and loved each other before?

She asked him if his arm still hurt, and he nodded. Her face had swollen even more overnight, and throbbed with a sharp, insistent pain.

As they neared Cornifu, Jennifer spoke from her place in the passenger seat.

"That's strange."

"What's strange," said Steven, "apart from everything that's happened to us the past two days?"

"We're almost back, and the road's been fine all the way."

"That figures," said Steven. "It makes about as much sense as anything else."

They arrived in front of the Cornifu Hotel, and Steven volunteered to go with Jennifer to see Bruce Campbell.

"I have to talk to him before we involve the police," she said.

"Maybe the hotel can find you a dentist," Steven said to Margaret, "and I'll see you as soon as I get back."

Margaret gave him the closest thing to a smile that her swollen face would allow before she turned into the hotel. Retrieving her key from the front desk, she went straight to her room, overwhelmingly grateful to be back amongst other people and familiar things. She turned on the television and found CNN debating the forthcoming election. The real world was still there. She went into the bathroom and soaked a face cloth in cold water, and just as she placed it carefully on her swollen face, she heard the television fall silent. Puzzled, she walked back into the room.

Bruce Campbell stood by the door, looking at her, a sardonic smile on his face.

She squealed in surprise, and dropped the cloth.

"How did you get in here?"

"I go where I please, Magda, my dear. You, of all people, should know that."

He spoke in English, but with a strange formality of expression unlike his former speech.

"What are you talking about, Bruce?" she said. "And who's Magda?"

"Oh dear," he said, with a mirthless laugh, "it seems you still don't know who you are. But then, you wouldn't, would you? It is only I who measure the lifetimes."

Margaret stared at him blankly.

"It has been three hundred-and-fifty years, Magda, but at long last I have what I want."

She felt the dark malevolence in his voice, and it chilled her to the very marrow of her bones. Sickening terror enveloped her in a paralyzing embrace. All the comforting familiarity of normal life, so recently restored, was swept away, and she felt lost and helpless.

He took as step closer, limping, and she backed away.

"Stay away from me."

"You have no conception, Magda," he said, fixing her with a stare so intense she felt transfixed. "No conception of how I have longed for this moment; the moment when I put an end to this tiresome and tedious cycle of repeating life. I shall be free of this damnable wound in my leg and the incessant pain of it."

Margaret took another step backwards. She was growing dizzy and afraid she might faint.

"Your father defied me, and I have killed him. Iuliana Banica, who wounded me, is dead as well. All that now remains is to kill that fool Serghei, and my revenge will be complete."

"You killed my father?" she said. "What did he ever do to you? He never met you until now."

"Foolish girl. But you will understand everything soon enough, my dear. You spurned me once, but you shall not do that again. When you are dead, as you will be as soon as I have finished with Serghei, I shall also be able to die. You and I will then be together forever, as I wished us to be so long ago. I will take your corpse to my tomb, and we shall lie side by side in blissful peace eternally."

He came closer still, and Margaret saw his eyes glowed a fiery red. She tried to back away, but found herself flat against the wall

"I know Serghei will come here," Campbell said. "The young cretin loves you, and you think you love him, but I shall triumph in the end, and you shall be mine."

A loud knocking on the door echoed in Margaret's ears, and she heard Steven's voice.

"Margaret, it's me. Open the door."

"I knew it," exulted Campbell.

"Steven," she screamed.

After two powerful kicks the door burst open, banging against the wall. Steven rushed in, closely followed by Jennifer. Campbell turned on them.

"Serghei Chisca," he hissed. "Finally. You escaped me at the castle, but you shall not escape me here."

Campbell prepared to lunge but Jennifer shouted, and he paused for an instant in apparent surprise.

"Stop, my lord."

Steven's hand flew upwards, and Margaret saw him press the wooden crucifix against Campbell's forehead. Campbell bellowed in pain and sank to his knees. The crucifix burned into his skull, until, with a final, agonized cry, he collapsed onto the floor. Margaret rushed into Steven's arms and watched in breathless horror and disbelief as the body before them aged and shriveled. It shrank and bent into the form of a withered old man, and then rapidly decomposed into a hideous, grinning skeleton. Its clothing rotted to nothing and its bones dried, cracked and crumbled into cold, dry dust.

The three of them stood staring at the white patches of powder on the dark brown carpet.

"Wow," breathed Jennifer. "Did you ever see anything like that before?"

"What is all this, please?" demanded the mystified and testy voice of the hotel manager from the open doorway, and the abrupt return to the here and now jolted Margaret like an electric shock.

"It's nothing now," said Steven. "Absolutely nothing at all."

* * * *

An hour later, Margaret, Steven and Jennifer sat in the hotel dining room sharing a bottle of wine.

"How's your face, Margaret?" asked Jennifer.

"Fine, thanks. The pain stopped the instant Campbell died. The swelling's all but gone now."

"Arm's fine, too," said Steven. "No problem."

"Thought so," said Jennifer.

"What do you mean?" asked Margaret. "Can you figure all this out?"

"I think so," said Jennifer, putting her wine glass down. "I learned a few new things."

"Like what?" asked Steven.

"When Steven the ghost buster went down to explore the cellars, I went to the library to get something to read. I thought I'd try for something on local history, but really old. I found a reprint of a late seventeenth century account of life in and around Cornifu. It's a personal journal really, kept by a priest named Father Crainic who ultimately became Archbishop of Bucharest. Quite a famous guy, but I never knew he kept a journal. Anyway, lo and behold, right there in that book, was an account of a wedding at which Crainic officiated when he was just a young country priest."

"And that told you what?" asked Margaret.

"Lord John wanted a local shepherd girl named Magda Arcos as a mistress…" Jennifer began.

"That *thing* upstairs called me Magda," interrupted Margaret, "and he said I was in love with someone called Serghei."

"Right," said Jennifer. "Magda refused to be John's mistress, and anyway she was betrothed to a boy named Serghei Chisca who worked in the kitchens at Erdely Castle. Lord John went to Magda's house and ordered her father to cancel the wedding and make Magda go to the castle, but he refused. A couple of nights later, Father Crainic married Magda and Serghei, but right after the ceremony a wolf came out of the forest and charged at the crowd. A woman named Iuliana Banica shot the wolf in the left hindquarter with a crossbow, and the wolf ran back into the forest. A hunting party was sent out, but they couldn't find the wolf, and Lord John was never seen again. The locals believed he was the wolf."

"Campbell called Steven Serghei Chisca, and he told me he'd killed Iuliana Banica," said Margaret, "but I don't see the connection."

"I didn't see any connection either, at first," said Jennifer. "Not until you started talking about your bad tooth and Steven told me about his arm."

She paused for another sip of wine.

"Neither Magda nor Serghei lived more than a few years after their wedding. Serghei fell off the roof of their house and broke his right arm. The injury killed him. Magda died less than a year later of an abscess that must have turned septic. Everyone said that Lord John had cursed them."

"Yes," said Steven, "I can see why they would think that, but all that happened to those people hundreds of years ago. Lord John didn't curse us."

"Actually, I think he did," Jennifer said.

"How?" said Margaret.

"I'll try to explain," said Jennifer. "You see, I'm pretty sure the curse Lord John called down on Magda and Serghei, and presumably the others as well, was called–roughly translated–the *Curse of a Hundred Lifetimes.*"

"I've read about that," said Steven. "It's a curse often associated with wandering spirits. People just keep on living, don't they? I'm beginning to get the picture."

"That's what Campbell said," put in Margaret. "Something about him being the only one who measures the lifetimes."

Jennifer nodded.

"The spirits of Magda and Serghei were forced by that curse to continue living, lifetime after lifetime. Lord John wanted his revenge, no matter how long it took."

"So you're saying that we're Magda and Serghei?" said Steven.

Jennifer nodded again.

"And if that's true," Steven went on, "that would explain why I thought I'd been in the castle cellars and why I thought the castle kitchen was familiar. Serghei worked in the kitchens and must have gone down into the cellars all the time."

"But what about Dad and Julia?" Margaret asked.

"Magda's father defied Lord John's orders, and he was cursed as well, but his fate was a little different. He lived an exceptionally long life, but he nearly went insane with terror having seen what happened to Magda and Serghei."

"Maybe that's why we had to persuade Dad to go to the castle," said Margaret. "His fear of Lord John. He said he had a feeling about Campbell, and the closer we got to the castle, the more frightened he was."

"So," said Steven, "that only leaves Julia, and she must have been that...er..."

"Iuliana Banica, who shot the wolf," said Jennifer. "Remember how Julia complained of being cold all the time? Well, it turns out that Iuliana died in a blizzard. The curse again. And her spirit lived on until Lord John could take revenge on her."

"Campbell's limp was the wolf's wound," said Margaret. "He said he'd been in pain for all those years."

"It all adds up," said Steven, finishing his wine. "But it's almost beyond belief. In fact, I still wouldn't have fully believed it if old Lord John hadn't dried up and blown away like he did."

"And there are your names as well," said Jennifer. "That only occurred to me when we got back to town. Magda Arcos, Margaret Archer. Serghei Chisca, Steven Chisholm. Iuliana Banica, Julia Baxter."

"And my father?" asked Margaret.

"Yes indeed," said Jennifer. "Magda's father was named Toma Arcos."

"Thomas Archer," whispered Margaret.

"Wow," said Steven.

Margaret sat silent for a time, absorbing what she had heard. She and Steven were alive, but Julia and her father had fallen victim to Lord John's ruthless revenge.

"I persuaded Dad to come on this trip," she said. "I led him right into this horror, and now he's dead."

"You couldn't have known," Steven said. "No one could. We were all brought here by a power none of us ever dreamed of, let alone understood. What happened to your father is not your fault."

Margaret looked at him, feeling an upwelling of affection that sprang from the very depths of her soul, and from a far-off and mist-shrouded time. He smiled at her, and then she turned to Jennifer again.

"What happens now, then?" she asked. "I mean this curse thing and all."

"The curse is broken," said Jennifer. "It must be. Lord John is truly dead and gone this time. He's not coming back, so you two are free. You can live normal lives. I'd say this is your final lifetime, in fact. This time, you're not coming back either."

"So we did know each other," said Margaret to Steven. "It wasn't our imagination."

Jennifer raised her wine glass with a smile.

"So, here's to Magda and Serghei. Finally free to live and love."

AUTHOR'S BIO:

Charles Mossop lives on Vancouver Island on Canada's Pacific coast where he retired after a thirty-two year career in post-secondary education. When not writing or editing he works with his wife, Louise, in their large garden and continues his study of classical guitar.

His historical fiction short stories have appeared in *Over My Dead Body,* *Futures Mystery Anthology Magazine* and in the Amazon Shorts section of Amazon.com. He has contributed to several anthologies including *The Muse on Writing (2005)* and *Aleatory's Junction (2006)*. His first novel, *Jade Hunter,* will be published in 2007 from Double Dragon Publishing. He is a member of the fiction editorial staff of *Mysterical-E* Magazine, as well as serving on editorial boards for non-fiction and educational materials.

We hope you've enjoyed The Carpathian Shadows: Volume I. Stay tuned for more eerie adventures and happenings at Lord John Erdely's Castle in Volume II... coming soon.

Lea Schizas

About the Editor:

Lea Schizas is an award-winning author/editor living in Montreal, Canada with her five children and husband. She edits for several publishing houses and in her spare time, when she finds spare time, she enjoys going to the movies or simply enjoying peace and quiet with a good book.

For more information, you can visit her website at: http://leaschizaseditor.com